The Club of Death

Banbury Cross Murder Mystery Series Book Two
Ben Westerham

I0545265

Also by Ben Westerham

BANBURY CROSS MURDER MYSTERY SERIES
The Hide and Seek Murders
The Club of Death
The Hobby Horse Murder
A Legacy of Death
The Golf Club Murder
Death of a Scarecrow

DAVID GOOD PRIVATE INVESTIGATOR SERIES
The Strawberry Girl
Good Investigations
Good Girl Gone Bad
Too Good to Die
Smart Way to Die
The Good Con
Good and the Vanishing Act
As Good As Dead

ALEXANDER TEMPLEMAN SPY THRILLER SERIES
The House of Spies
The Meyer-Hoffman Affair

SHORTS IN THE DARK SERIES
Harry Minch

Memory of Murder
Lesson for a Thief
Collector of Crimes (anthology)
Shattered Dreams (anthology)

50FOR30 SERIES OF MICRO SHORT STORIES
50for30 Series One
50for30 Series Two

MULTI-AUTHOR ANTHOLOGIES
Breakneck

This story is a work of fiction and any resemblance
to people and places is purely coincidental.

To my Godparents, Sylvia and Peter Bones,
who always make me smile.

It's all English to me

A word on the language that's used in this book, so you know what to expect. The version of English that is used here is British. This ought not to present much in the way of a problem for non-British readers. If you do find the occasional word or phrase a little odd, then I hope you still understand the essence of what is being said.

Ride a cock-horse to Banbury Cross

Ride a cock-horse to Banbury Cross,
To see a fine lady upon a white horse;
With rings on her fingers and bells on her toes,
She shall have music wherever she goes.

This is a typical modern version of the popular nursery rhyme.
There are numerous earlier recorded versions that start with
the same opening line.

Chapter One

Henry Graball was aglow with the flush of success. Hardly a novel experience to him, but a most satisfying one all the same. The room he surveyed from his vantage point at the bar was packed with the great and good of Banbury, every single invitation he'd issued having received a positive response. Hardly surprising, he reminded himself, since none of the hopeless, toadying bunch would have dared to risk turning him down. They'd be far too afraid of upsetting him. And there were very few people indeed who could afford to do such a thing. His reach, he knew, was too great for any to escape his influence. He'd brought down business empires, seen councillors removed from office and even brought a premature end to a marriage or two in his time; a rather remarkable tally of achievements, he mused.

The late afternoon party at the Banbury Conservative Club was ostensibly to celebrate the twenty-fifth anniversary of North Oxfordshire Engineering, the crown in his extensive network of businesses. But in reality, the occasion gave him a bloody good opportunity to flaunt his wealth to all and sundry. And why not, when he'd worked so damn hard to acquire it? Rub their noses in it, that's what he liked to do. Remind them just how much he'd got and how very little they had.

He'd taken advantage of a downturn in the business fortunes of a competitor in 1937 to snap up the assets and customers for a trivial price, then merged them with his own business. The war years had been good to him. Already middle-aged and suffering from a back problem he'd been able to exaggerate to a significant degree, he'd been able to avoid getting called up, instead spending the odd morning or afternoon creeping around the nearby countryside as part of the Home Guard.

This provided him with plenty of time to make the most of his growing network of acquaintances to extend his business reach. Some came to him willingly, others less so, prompted by a sudden desire to avoid having a little, or not so little, indiscretion unmasked. By the time the fighting was over, his business empire was ten times the size it had been six years earlier and he was already one of the town's leading lights.

There were a few survivors of those early days in the room with him now. Brian Crown, his former accountant, had a creative streak entirely unexpected in one of his kind. Graball had never been able to find another with the same flair for invention and imagination. He'd rewarded Crown well, providing enough for the money man and his wife to buy a modest mansion in one of the villages south of the town. They still met for afternoon tea every few weeks, enjoying the opportunity to reminisce.

Matthew Louch was cowering in the far corner, attempting to hide behind that skinny wife of his. The pathetic man had once been leader of the town council, but he'd dared to deny planning permission for one of Graball's property schemes, a masterly plan to build upmarket homes along the south bank of the River Cherwell. Something about heritage buildings, or so they'd said. Louch had never liked him, he'd always known that, and he had never forgiven the weasel-faced man for blocking his ambitions. He'd taken his revenge by financing an extensive investigation into Louch's campaign funding at the subsequent elections. The findings hadn't been positive. Something of a surprise to the good councillor, by all accounts, who had to resign forthwith. Happy days.

"Ah, Henry, there you are. Hiding away as usual. Your guests are most anxious to offer you their congratulations. You should mingle more," said a voice to his left.

The slender, wrinkled-faced woman wearing a tiara and a long lime-green dress from several decades past, was Julia Bothington. Her family had once been extensive landowners and members of the Home Counties aristocracy, but most of the wealth had been lost in the years between the wars, the result of some God-awful investments made by her father. Graball tolerated her as a means of reminding himself just how far he had come and how far others had fallen. He suspected she hung around him in the hope of picking up the occasional hand-out. If she did, she had been continually disappointed.

"Don't know why I invited them all in the first place," he growled. "They're only here for the free food and drink. Look at them, gorging themselves on everything they can get their hands on. Parasites, every last one of 'em."

"Now, now. We can't have you bad tempered today. That really won't do. Even if we are all a bunch of hangers-on, this is your party and you should jolly well enjoy it," Julia Bothington cajoled.

He looked at the woman, who was staring at him in a way that reminded him of an old schoolteacher, stern and expecting a positive response. Maybe she was right. The old dear did talk sense sometimes. He took a pull on the stump of a cigar he'd been nursing for quite some time and let the thick, peaty smoke escape through his nostrils before speaking again.

"I don't suppose you've seen where that wife of mine has got to? Least she could do would be to take a turn round the room with her husband."

"I think you'll find she's already ahead of you there," replied Julia Bothington, pointing a thin pale finger in the direction of the McKinnons. "Now, what on earth made you decide to invite those two? She really is such a terrible gossip."

"I didn't. Daphne did," he grumbled.

He stubbed out the remains of his cigar and picked up his glass of whisky. It was already his third of the day. A man needed fortification if he was going to have to be civil to so many people, all at the same time. Probably ought to have kept the bottle. Good God, what a prospect, shaking hand after hand, agreeing on how bloody wonderful the weather was for the time of year, or being told for the umpteenth time how remarkable his achievements had been. As if he needed telling.

"Well, I suppose there's no avoiding it," he announced, steeling himself for what was to follow.

"That's the spirit," Julia Bothington responded, tapping him on the arm with one of her thin, veiny hands.

"IT'S BEEN TWENTY-FIVE years of hard bloody graft, and don't you doubt that. I started with bugger all. No advantages in life, not like some of you here. I've done it all myself. Blood, sweat and tears, morning, noon and night. There's been those what have tried to knock me down and there's been the naysayers, idiots who think everything in life is impossible. But I've overcome the lot of 'em. And look where I am now, worth millions, with one of the biggest businesses across the whole of Oxfordshire. But take it from the horse's mouth, I'm not finished yet. If you're one of those hoping I'm about to bugger off into a quiet retirement and leave the field open, then you can bloody well think again. If I have my way, there's another twenty-five years to come and I plan on turning North Oxfordshire Engineering into a national player, one of the titans of the industry, capable of delivering the biggest contracts here and overseas."

Henry Graball stood behind a lectern on a small, raised platform positioned at one end of the dining hall, looking out over more than forty attentive faces. They'd just finished their main course of roasted lamb and it was his moment to say a few words. He hadn't really wanted to, not if it meant he had to hold his tongue and avoid adding a few home truths to what he said. But his fellow directors and even his wife, the ever thoughtful Daphne, had insisted on it. It was, they all said, the reason everyone would be there, to hear him speak and to show their appreciation for all he had done.

Appreciation? What a farce. There were people out there, clustered around circular tables in half-dozen packs, who would stab him in the back and spit on his grave if they got half a chance. Hypocrites, liars, leeches. And there they were, all smiles, pretending there was nothing else they'd rather be doing than sitting here listening to him as if he was Isambard Kingdom Brunel. That giant of the engineering world wouldn't have put up with it. No, he'd have kicked them out and half-way down the street.

The muscles in the back of his calves ached. He wanted to sit back down and stretch out his legs, but he wasn't about to let that lot see any sign of weakness. They'd fall on him like a pack of starving wolves. His success had been built on strength: strength of mind and strength of character, and he wasn't going to waver now.

The room, though large enough to easily accommodate the party, was not well ventilated. Only one of the windows had been opened, for fear the noise from the street below and the fumes from the passing traffic would prove an inconvenience. Graball felt a bead of sweat roll down his spine and settle in the crease of his shirt, where it tucked into his trousers. August had been a warm month, even more so than July. Fine in many ways, but not so for an indoor function. He resisted the temptation to loosen his collar.

His wife sat at the far side of the table, immediately opposite him, flanked by the town mayor and his wife on one side and the chairman of the Conservative Club and his wife on the other. He might have smiled at Daphne, in other circumstances. She looked bloody good in that bright red dress that showed off her sexy shoulders and slender arms. They'd always been one of her best features, those shoulders. It calmed his mind to run his hands over the firm, smooth skin, along the line of the bone to those beautifully round shoulders. He was a fortunate man, really, even if it was still true to say he brought more to the party than she did, so to speak.

Her lips weren't as plush as they used to be, but they still felt good pressed up against his own. And she'd kept her figure better than most women her age. He'd chosen well, despite his reservations at the time. One of the best deals he'd managed to close over the years.

But that look on her face was a familiar one. Something was bothering her. The little pinch of her nose and the crease in the skin above it. She was trying to speak to him, tell him something wasn't quite right. But she didn't need to speak to get her message across, not after all these years. She was telling him to be nicer to his guests, say how wonderful they all were and how hugely grateful he was they'd decided to show up for all the free food and booze they could manage. And there was still another hour to go. He dug the nail of each thumb into the side of the matching index finger and looked back up to re-engage the masses.

"But it wouldn't be right of me to claim all the credit for myself, or not quite all of it," he resumed, scratching the side of his nose with the tip of one finger, leaving a pause for each of his guests to wonder if it might be them who was about to get a pat on the back. Fat chance.

"A man like me needs a good woman at home. One who's always there, rain or shine, to provide a solid base for him to operate from. And I've been fortunate enough to be married for the past twenty-three years to one of the best women a man could possibly hope to call his own. She's raised three children for me, seeing them all safely out into the world; even when they were reluctant to bugger off. She runs our home like a well-oiled machine, never complaining or needing to be pampered every minute of the day, unlike many I could point a finger at."

A gentle and rather uneasy murmur of amusement arose from the audience. Graball gave them their moment, then pressed on.

"Yes, I'd like to thank my darling wife, Daphne, for putting up with me all these years. You're a credit to your sex, my love, and a better example for others to follow it wouldn't be possible to find. For my wife," he went on, raising his glass towards the audience. "A blessing in my life."

Barks of approval were accompanied by a sea of upheld glasses, followed in short order by a round of applause.

Daphne Graball tilted her head to one side, so as to more easily exchange a word or two with the Mayor's wife, while smiling sweetly at her husband. She hadn't been expecting him to say anything about her; after all, the celebration was a business one and she had never had any involvement whatsoever in Henry's business affairs. Even if she was ever to have expressed an interest, it was highly unlikely he would have encouraged her involvement. He'd always made it clear he liked to keep a firm divide between business and the home, as if he feared one might contaminate the other.

But she very much doubted her husband had the foggiest idea how hard it had been for her while he spent practically every waking hour at work. The children hardly knew their father, the poor things, despite her best efforts to encourage him to take a bigger role in their upbringing. And she had spent so little time with him after the first two or three years of their marriage that she'd become used to him not being around. Home was her domain, one into which Henry wandered like a lost sheep from time to time. It had not been the life she had expected at the outset.

He'd taken care of her and the children, that was true enough, but she had yearned for more intimacy, more expressions of love. For him so say something like that now, in such a public forum, was wonderful. It made her heart soar and it took a little effort to hold back the tears. He wouldn't like that, crying, even if they were tears of joy. She could share those with him later.

"And here's to another twenty-five successful years for North Oxfordshire Engineering," boomed Henry.

Outright cheers this time, mingled with calls of congratulation from the obedient congregation. He soaked up their pathetic adoration for a moment, before stepping down from the lectern to join his beloved wife. He had, he felt certain, delivered a first-class sermon.

IT WAS AS COFFEE WAS being served that a member of the club staff handed Graball a small silver plate, on which was placed a single folded piece of paper. He opened up the paper and read its contents, so brief it took mere seconds.

"You'll have to excuse me for a moment or two, ladies and gentlemen," he announced to those sitting round his table. "I need to take a phone call. Seems it's urgent and you can never keep business waiting."

"You won't be long, will you, my love. Only I know the Mayor has a wonderful speech to deliver about you," said Daphne.

She held the fingers of her husband's hand in her own, her upturned face radiant with joy. A delightful tingle ran up her spine as Graball leaned down and kissed her lightly on the forehead.

"No need to worry, my dear. I'll be back shortly."

As he marched across the room, his long, straight-legged strides eating up the ground, those he passed raised a glass or shook his hand, eager, it appeared, to underline their congratulations. He met each with nothing more than a curt nod of the head.

"Never misses an opportunity to make a bit of money, that husband of yours," quipped Nigel Nettle, the Banbury mayor, with a chuckle.

"Oh, you can say that again, Nigel, dear," jumped in Anne Nettle, the mayor's wife, whose copious head of dyed black hair was beginning to look a little dishevelled, with some of the many clips that held it in place beginning to work their way lose. "The man should be running the Exchequer. The country wouldn't have any money worries if he did, don't you agree, Daphne, darling?"

Daphne Graball found the large woman sitting on the other side of the table a little too loud for own tastes. It wasn't that the mayoress was unpleasant, nor that she couldn't be entertaining company. It was just that she was so loud and over-powering it left little space, even in such a large room, for anyone else. Perhaps that was why she had married such a small man; he didn't take up much room.

"I don't doubt for a moment, Anne, that Henry would jump at the chance to tell the Government how to run the country. Though I'm not sure that would necessarily be a good thing."

"Oh, rubbish," cut in Anne Nettle, taking care to ensure she had the full attention of all those seated around their table. "He'd jolly well sort them out. Spend, spend, spend is all those politicians seem to do. About time someone showed them how to manage a budget properly, Don't you agree Phillip? Henry would soon sort them out."

Phillip Underwood, chairman of the Banbury Conservative Association and director of an Oxford-based insurance company, didn't appreciate his fellow guest's brazen attempt at dragging him into a silly conversation that had no practical point whatsoever. Henry Graball would never be Chancellor of the Exchequer, nor get the opportunity to enlighten the Exchequer with the dubious benefit of his opinions as to how they should go about their work. In any case, it was entirely likely that, should Graball get anywhere near Government office, he wouldn't settle for a minor post. No, he would aim his sights at the top job, prime minister. He doubted, too, that a woman as remarkable and caring as Daphne Graball would wish to entertain such a conversation. Really, why did she put up with that self-centred, arrogant husband of hers. The man never paid her the attention she deserved, yet expected her to jump to it whenever he chose to snap his fingers. If only he had met Daphne long before Graball did. Life could have been so very different for the two of them.

"I should imagine a man as ambitious as Henry would be very unlikely to settle for minor office. He's the sort who wouldn't stop at anything short of Number 10," asserted Philippa Underwood, her fleshy, round face dappled with perspiration.

She wasn't enjoying herself. For one thing, she was too warm. She had told her husband more than once in the past that he should have more windows installed in the club's main function room. It was far from being the first time she'd found herself sitting in the room on a hot day coated in a film of perspiration. As usual, Phillip had done his level best to ignore her. She was also unimpressed they were sharing a table with the Graballs; although, given her husband's status, it was not altogether a surprise. Phillip's ridiculous infatuation with Daphne Graball was as old as it was tiresome. The wonder was, that Henry Graball seemed to be blissfully unaware of it. Silly man.

"Absolutely," enthused Anne Nettle. "Perhaps we should start a campaign, what do you think?"

"Graball for Westminster," said her husband, drawing an imaginary banner in the air over the table. "We could be on to a winner."

"I see little enough of him now," replied Daphne Graball. "If he went into politics, I'd likely see nothing of him at all."

Phillipa Underwood was tempted to suggest that might be a good thing, but decided against it. Whilst she would herself not mind in the slightest if she saw nothing of her husband for long periods of time, it seemed most unlikely Daphne Graball felt the same way about Henry. She doted on him to an alarming extent; well beyond what was reasonable, given how little attention he seemed to give her in return.

It did occur to her that her feelings on the subject were really just a manifestation of a little jealousy on her part, regarding Daphne's apparent happiness. Not jealousy in an unpleasant way. She didn't want to take away the other woman's pleasure. No, she longed to feel something of the sort herself. It had all seemed so, well, promising when she'd taken that long, slow walk down the aisle of Belchington Church. Phillip looked so handsome in his uniform and so pleased to be there. There had been a moment, several months before the wedding, when he'd seemed a little uncertain, but that had passed and the day had gone so well. A bright and beautiful life lay ahead of them. But somewhere, when and where she'd never been able to identify, things had started to go wrong. A little argument here, a small silence there. A late arrival for dinner or a forgotten social engagement. They all built up, until... She didn't really know where she stood now. Even maintaining a public appearance of contentment had become difficult. The future was a fog through which she could glimpse not a thing.

"Ah, yes, you could be right about that," smiled Nigel Nettle.

"There again, you could set up home with him in London. Imagine the shops and the shows. And the people you'd meet. Prime ministers, kings, queens, film stars. Oh, yes, film stars. How exciting. Perhaps Nigel could get a job in the Cabinet, too," laughed Anne Nettle with a little rock of the head.

"Slow down, dear. I'm happy enough where I am, thanks very much," replied her husband.

MATTHEW LOUCH STILL wasn't sure why they were really there, celebrating with Henry Graball and his many, many cronies. The man was as disgusting a human-being as he'd ever met and treated everyone he came into contact with in the same obnoxious way. Even his so-called friends seemed to be nothing more than a convenient means of building up his business empire. People were expendable, in the eyes of Henry Graball.

He had asked his wife, Sheila, why she was so set on going to the party of a man who had been responsible for putting an end to his burgeoning political career. As far as he was concerned, he'd rather be licking stinging nettles than applauding Graball. But Sheila had been insistent. They were going to accept the invitation. They had to take every chance that came their way to mix in the right circles, she had insisted. It had been hard enough, she said, to keep any of their friends after what Graball had done and they couldn't afford to miss such a good opportunity to hang on to those threadbare relationships.

Even as he'd flopped out of bed that morning, he'd held on to a lingering hope Sheila would change her mind, deciding it wasn't such a good idea after all; but she hadn't wavered. She never did, not when she'd made her mind up about something. He ought to have realised that. And she was right. Either they had to patch things up, re-establish themselves in the eyes of others, or else leave and start all over again somewhere else. Neither of them were keen on that. Why should they be?

At least Graball hadn't paid them any attention since they'd arrived. Christ knows how he would be able to look the man in the eye and say something nice about him. Some of the other guests had been lukewarm towards them, but the rest had been alright. Or, at the very least, civil. Most people there knew it was Graball who was responsible for his downfall and that seemed to help. Most likely, the majority of people in the room had suffered in some way or other at the hands of Graball, which meant they'd be more understanding than most of the Banbury population.

But listening to the man's self-centred, egotistical speech flicked some sort of switch inside him. It made him angry, more angry than he'd been since Graball's hounds had passed on their little dossier to the local paper, which had not wasted a moment turning it into a front-page story. 'Council leader in funding scandal' was never going to look good. He'd been forced to step down before the day was over. The shame and embarrassment were followed by anger and frustration. Then, after a while, by an overwhelming sense of being helpless and without hope.

And Sheila, as his wife, she'd had to bear the suffering too. That was unfair. He'd had nothing to do with the irregularities that Graball's people had unearthed and she was even further removed from events. That didn't stop people from giving Sheila a hard time. Guilt by association, so it seemed. She'd been up to maintaining a brave and determined face in public but in private she'd struggled for a time, angry and tearful by turns. It took months for things to settle down and their lives to return to anything like normal, but since then she'd been determined they weren't going to let that be an end to things.

She'd been a dynamo, pushing him on, trying to get him to recover some of the lost ground, reluctant though he was to even show his face in public.

But Graball's speech made it sound like the whole bloody world owed him a favour. And the way he set himself out to be some sort of industrial titan, commanding armies of workers and raking in more money than he knew what to do with. It was disgusting. It made his blood boil to listen to that and if he got the chance he was going to let Graball know exactly what he thought of him, preferably in front of the entire room.

When Louch saw Graball leaving the room, it was too good an opportunity to miss. Telling his wife he was going to the toilet, he slipped round the outside of the other tables and through the same doorway as Graball had used, so focused on his mission that all the other sights, sounds and smells in the packed room made no further impression on him.

He entered a wide corridor and, as he went to turn a corner at the end, Louch spotted Graball some way up ahead, talking in a most animated fashion with a member of the club staff. Both had their voices raised, though not quite sufficiently for him to hear what they were saying, apart from the odd word every now and again. Why should he be surprised if Graball was laying into a member of the staff just like he did everyone else? The poor man had probably committed some heinous crime, like not holding the door open for the most important man in the world.

Louch kept himself just out of sight from the other two, trying to make out the cause of the fuss. As he watched, an odd thought occurred to him. If he didn't know better, he'd say the two arguing men knew each other. There was something about their behaviour, a familiarity perhaps, that suggested they were already acquainted. Not that it was ever likely to make a difference to Graball whether or not he knew someone, if he felt inclined to set about them. As far as he was concerned, every other human being on the planet was fair game.

It was very frustrating he couldn't get any closer without giving himself away. If only he could make out what it was they were damned well arguing about. It might prove to be something useful. But there again, perhaps it was too late now to go looking for something that might give him a hold, even a small one, over Graball. The only truly satisfying outcome he could think of now, the only one he'd been happy to imagine for months, was Graball's death. Better still if it was a horrible, drawn-out and painful death.

Whatever the two men had been arguing over, their row came to an abrupt end and it was no surprise that Graball appeared to have emerged the winner. The other man's shoulders slumped and he nodded his head as he looked down at the floor. Graball, the condescending piece of filth, gave him a pat on the shoulder, in the manner of someone who had just delivered some awful news. Louch felt his palms grow sweaty and he struggled to hold back the urge to intervene.

From somewhere further down the corridor came the sound of other voices. People were approaching. Graball looked up, appeared to see whoever was heading his way, brushed the shoulder of the staff member's jacket with his right hand as he said something more to him, then set off down the corridor, out of sight. As if released from some inhuman trap and keen to get as far away as possible, as quickly as he could, the other man hurried towards Louch, as if responding to a starting pistol. Louch, almost caught out by the suddenness of events, straightened his back and started to walk forwards, eager to make it appear as if he had only just arrived on the scene.

Should he stop the staff member and quiz him, Louch wondered? He might have information about Graball that could prove useful. It was a tempting idea, for a moment, but he had already made up his mind. He would let the other man pass unmolested and continue his pursuit of Graball. Seconds later, the two men exchanged a brief nod of the head and disappeared out of each other's sight.

STANDING ON THE PAVEMENT in the shade of an old chestnut tree that loomed over the front of the Conservative Club, was a lone woman, drawing heavily on a cigarette she had only just lit. Half a dozen cigarettes lay like half-squashed corpses on the ground around her feet, all of them discarded almost as soon as they had been started. She took repeated little steps on the spot and her heavily made-up face wore an expression of concern.

Wendy Slip threw her latest cigarette to the ground, grinding the lit end under-foot with the same impatience she had with the others, then retrieved a compact mirror from her brown leather handbag and held it in front of her face. She had gone to some lengths before leaving home to ensure she looked as good as she'd ever done, but the train journey up from Oxford and the walk from Banbury station had left her worried she wouldn't still look as good.

She fiddled with her shoulder-length, jet black hair, cut only the day before, then touched up her bright red lips, nervous fingers struggling to keep a grip on the metallic lipstick tube before she returned it to her bag. Henry Graball liked her to look her very best, whatever the circumstances. Even when they'd finished making love, he would expect her to tidy up her hair and her make-up. If she was to have any chance of persuading him to change his mind, to take her back, she would have to look irresistible.

Two large, elderly gentlemen ambled in through the entrance to the old Turkish baths on the opposite side of the road, while three crows flapped and squawked in disagreement over the remains of a single chip on the kerb some twenty yards away. If she had not been there with a particular purpose, it would have been nice to sit on a bench in the sun, letting its rays play over her skin.

She looked again at her watch, not really taking any notice of the time it told, checked her handbag was properly closed, then, shoulders rising as she took a deep breath, turned on her high-heels, walked up the steps to the club's entrance and went in through the open doorway. She was nervous, but there was no point in hanging around like a wet lettuce. She had to do something, before it was too late. The buxom, blonde slut who'd taken her place as Henry's mistress had already been moved into a flat. It wouldn't be long before he'd insist she, herself, clear out of the flat he'd been paying for over the last two years. The prospect made her shudder.

It was easy to talk her way past the young man on reception. She had learned how to take advantage of hungry young men like that a long time ago. Look helpless and timid, so they can feel they are coming to your rescue, then tease them with some flesh by undoing an extra button on the front of her blouse. This one was so hopeless he nearly tripped over his own feet when he rushed to open the door giving her access to the stairway.

Where to look next was the problem. The receptionist had told her Henry's party was in the main hall; up the stairs, then through the double-doors on the left and follow the corridor all the way round. She couldn't miss it. But she didn't want to speak to Henry in public. He'd blow a gasket if his wife saw them together. She needed to get him to meet her somewhere private. It wouldn't take long. She just needed a little time alone with him; to make him see sense.

Why had she made such a stupid mess of things when he'd told her he wanted to end their relationship? Why? She should have kept her head and shown him why he was making such a silly mistake. Everybody makes a silly mistake now and then. It's only human. Henry would see that, if only she could get him to herself for five minutes. That was all, just five minutes.

Her heart was racing and she could feel her breathing was shallow. Calm down. Breathe properly. She sucked in big lungfuls of air as she stood at the bottom of the stairs. That was better. She needed to be calm and in control of herself if she was going to be able to do things properly. It was the most important thing she'd ever done and she was going to get it right, this time.

As she placed a foot on the bottom step, Wendy Slip heard voices from the floor above, followed by the clip of shoes on the stairs. She took half-a-dozen steps, forcing herself to smile and to give off the appearance of someone who belonged at the club. But her progress was stopped in its tracks by a familiar and oh-so-wonderful voice.

"Wendy, what the hell are you doing here, for God's sake? I thought I'd made myself perfectly clear last week. We're over. Done. Finished."

Henry Graball stood half-a-dozen steps above her, his right hand on the thick oak railing, his cheeks tinged with red as if he'd been exerting himself. His words were spoken with a good deal of undisguised anger. The bloody woman should not be there. It might well cause him a hell of a lot of trouble if anyone saw them together. He'd have to get rid of her right away, or at least as soon as he'd taken this phone call. Bloody hell, as if the day wasn't unpleasant enough, now he had something else to sort out.

"Henry, darling. I've been missing you. I wanted to..."

"Never mind that, you need to get out of here before someone sees us."

He thumped down the final few steps and grabbed her right arm, pushing her around so that she nearly tumbled down the stairs. His fingers bit hard, making her gasp with pain.

"Henry, that hurts."

"Down the stairs, you stupid woman. I can't believe it."

He wanted to shout, scream even, but that would only draw attention. Get her outside, on the street, and into a taxi as soon as possible. Anger bubbled up inside him, threatening a loss of self-control he knew he'd regret. It was hard to keep a lid on it. He'd paid her off generously. Given her a month to find a new home. Even told her she could take all the furniture from the flat he'd been paying for. What had he done to deserve this?

"But Henry, I love you." They nearly fell again as they reached the bottom step. "Surely you still love me?"

"Love? What do you mean, love? You were my bit on the side. Casual sex when I felt like it. You've got hold of the wrong end of the stick, you idiot. What the hell gave you the idea I was in love?"

For a moment she was tempted to burst into tears. How had she got it so wrong? How had she allowed herself to be used like this? But almost as soon as the feeling appeared, it left her again, to be replaced by a new one. A very different one. She felt a cold calm fill her body and a new idea fill her head. If he really meant what he said, she wasn't going to take that lying down. No, she'd see to it that he paid for deceiving her like that.

She threw off his grip on her arm and staggered across the hallway towards a closed door. Before he could reach her, she had opened it and fallen through, into a small, cluttered office. He followed her inside and, as he did so, she turned towards him, her eyes so full of anger that he was, for a moment, taken aback.

"No, Henry, you are not going to throw me away as easily as that."

OWEN PLENTY HAD SLIPPED out of the function room just before Henry Graball stood up to give his little speech. The prospect had been sickening. No doubt the self-centred money-grabbing man intended to take the opportunity to remind them all how bloody marvellous he was. A titan of the industrial world. Did it all by himself. No mention of those who'd run themselves into the ground for him or the bodies that littered the way. It made his stomach turn to think that he'd once looked upon the man as a friend and mentor. How blind could he have been? Some had warned him to take care, but he'd carried on all the same, oblivious to the true nature of the beast. God, what an idiot he'd been.

He'd taken the stairs to the top floor, where a small landing with a pair of chairs gave a view over the rear of the club, a mishmash of yards and roof tops. It was quiet there and he needed the space to himself. Time to cool off, before he did something stupid, like punch the bloody man's lights out. God, the temptation was strong. It wasn't as if Graball didn't deserve some kind of pay-back for what he'd done.

Plenty drew heavily on a cigarette and hammered the arm of his chair with his other hand. Stupid, stupid, stupid. He should have listened, not been so desperately keen. And the worst of it was, there was absolutely nothing he could do about it now. He'd realised his mistake far too late.

Voices drifted up from below, but they held no interest for him. Other matters weighed on his mind, heavy and persistent. They'd given him sleepless nights and frayed his nerves for days, leaving him bad-tempered, thick-headed and unable to focus properly on his work.

It seemed that, like so many others before him, he'd found out the hard way just what sort of a man Henry Graball was. Gross and ignorant in the extreme. So utterly self-centred and without feeling or consideration for others. He'd probably be perfectly happy if every other human being on the planet dropped dead, except then he'd have no one to buy his goods. Men like him were a blight. A plague on the rest of humanity.

The voices from below grew louder, one a woman's, the other a man's. They seemed to be involved in a disagreement. He had no idea who the woman might be, but he recognised the man. Plenty got to his feet and peered over the banister, taking care not to draw attention to himself. Henry Graball was standing towards the bottom of the stairs, waving a hand at a dark-haired woman as he spoke. It was hard to make out whole sentences and the woman's voice hardly carried at all, but Graball seemed very annoyed she was there.

Plenty's mind raced. There had been rumours, from more than one quarter, that Graball wasn't exactly faithful to his wife. Talk about a mistress had surfaced every once in a while, normally when drink was present, but he'd written it off as idle gossip, the sort of thing you always get where someone with a public profile as high as Graball's was concerned.

On the other hand, it was the kind of behaviour you'd expect of the man. He was probably conceited enough to think he had a right to keep another woman on the side. Perhaps, just perhaps, he'd stumbled on to an opportunity, a possible way out of his predicament.

He stubbed out his cigarette in the metal ashtray on the table and glanced again over the banister, before making his way down the stairs, treading with care so that the two people still arguing in the hallway wouldn't hear him coming. A thin smile grew on his face.

Chapter Two

Inspector Leslie Dykeman was no mean bar billiards player and racking up a decent score was never a serious challenge. But there was no getting away from the fact that his sergeant, Stanley Shapes, was the best player at the police station. Even when the grumpy oik was feeling under the weather, or under the influence, he had an impressive knack of being able to pull a big score out of the air when he needed it.

The pair of them had spent the best part of an hour, since scoffing down their lunchtime sandwiches, going head-to-head against constables Dartington and Squirrel, both of whom weren't half bad at the game themselves. In fact, it had been Squirrel who'd persuaded the powers that be to set up a bar billiards table in the rest room in the first place. A fine piece of toadying up to the Chief Inspector, that had been, as far as Dykeman was concerned.

As they headed into the final game, Dykeman had felt the pressure, messing up several attempted pots. Their two quid stake money had been in serious jeopardy, an unsatisfactory state of affairs neither he nor Shapes were accustomed to experiencing, seeing how their usual tactic was to only risk such sums when they were totally confident of winning.

Happily for them and unfortunately for the two constables, Shapes had stepped up to the plate and rattled up a massive score. Dartington was now left with the prospect of having to score a maximum if he and Squirrel were to avoid losing. The tension was palpable. There had been nothing like it since Derby Day, when Shapes had missed out on a fortune in the final race, when the last horse in his six-way accumulator had been overhauled in the closing hundred yards, eventually coming in a measly third. The poor man had been left distraught.

Dartington bent down over the cue, sliding it back and forth in the groove between his forefinger and thumb. His feet were set wide apart, his backside pointing towards the ceiling. Shapes burped. Dartington ignored him. Dykeman coughed. Dartington ignored that, too. Fingers twitched, brows were furrowed and tongues licked at dry lips.

'Get on with it man', Dykeman wanted to shout out. Dartington never had been the fastest gun in the West. Maybe he could cause a distraction, then give the constable's elbow a bit of a shove. Possible. But the odds were against him getting away with it. No, they'd just have to wait and see.

At last, in the wash of sunlight that spilled in from the window nearest the green baize, the cue moved back and forth one last time, followed by the solid, familiar sound of contact with the white ball. Dykeman watched it roll eagerly down the length of the table, Dartington not moving an inch as he too tried to establish whether or not he'd got his angles right. Shapes sucked in air noisily in the manner of a builder preparing to give his prospective client a quote for work.

'Damn, it looks a good 'un', thought Dykeman. Squirrel must have thought the same, as he let out a yelp of encouragement. But was it? Squirrel had gone for the trickiest shot on the table. Dykeman had mucked it up himself several times. Only Squirrel and Shapes had shown they had what it took to score a maximum consistently. The ball leapt back off the top cushion at an impressive angle, rolling ever more slowly towards the hole.

"Go on," screamed Squirrel, slapping a hand on Dartington's shoulder.

"No chance," snarled Shapes, rubbing a hand over his stubbled chin.

The ball closed on the hole. It looked good for a score. Damn it, thought Dykeman, they were going to lose. The shame. The loss of cash. He rolled his fingers into his palms. But no, the shot wasn't perfect after all. The ball rolled round the lip of the hole, then trundled on, into the pin, which tumbled to the baize, as if it wanted nothing more than a nice rest. Victory! Winnings! Dartington's head slumped forward on to the edge of the table.

"Nice try, mate," offered Squirrel. "I thought it was in."

Since it wasn't the done thing at the station to jump up and down with joy, Dykeman and Shapes settled for a handshake, first between themselves, then with their defeated opponents. They'd save the cheap jibes and sneers for another time, when they needed something to fall back on. Neither man, however, could keep a huge grin from appearing on his face.

"Well done, Shapes. I left you with plenty to do there," said Dykeman.

"Yeah, you were rubbish, sir."

"Nice game, sir. You too, sergeant," offered Squirrel. "I really thought we'd got you there."

If he was feeling deflated, Squirrel was doing a good job of hiding it, decided Dykeman. That was to his credit. Couldn't stand a sore loser, unless he was that loser.

"I thought you'd got it, too," replied the Inspector.

As money changed hands, at Shapes's eager behest, and cues were replaced on their rack, the scene of the titanic sporting engagement was interrupted by the appearance in the open doorway of another figure. Dykeman looked across at the clearly excited figure.

"What is it, Crouch? Something to say?"

"Certainly have, sir."

The man had something to say and it would help them all if he got on with it sooner rather. Crouch's eyes were aglow, like mini-fires, dancing with excitement. He looked, thought Dykeman, like a small child who'd just found his first frog and run inside to tell his parents. Well, he was young. He'd grow up, eventually.

"Well, get on with then," prodded the Inspector.

"Murder, sir. It's a murder."

Shapes stared at the wide-eyed constable, who looked like he was about to break out into some sort of dance, and felt an urge to pull his ear or kick him up the backside. Where did they get them from? Straight out the nursery, if you asked him. Their mums probably still tucked them in when they went to bed at night.

"Who's been topped and where, Crouch?" demanded Shapes, his eyes narrowing.

"Er," wavered Crouch, casting an eye over a small scrap of paper he held in a vice-like grip. "Henry Graball. At the Conservative Club. The Chief Inspector wants you on the case, sir," he added, looking back at Dykeman.

"Graball? I know that name," replied Dykeman. "He's that tycoon. The one who goes around like he owns the whole town and half the county."

"He owns North Oxfordshire Engineering, sir," chipped in Shapes. "Got more money than the Queen, or so he keeps telling people. From what I've heard, there's a long list of people who'd feel like they've got a good reason to bump him off."

Dykeman's face had gone blank. He was deep in thought and the thoughts he was having weren't all happy ones. He smelled danger. A great big, stinking pile of danger.

"Something up, sir?" asked Shapes.

"Yes, there's plenty up. This is one case I don't much fancy. All those big-wigs; politicians and businessmen. They'll all be expecting to get special treatment. We put so much as a little toe out of place and there's going to be a good chance it gets chopped off. I don't like the look of this one at all."

IN THE CAR, ON THE way across town to the Conservative Club, Dykeman elaborated on why he was so bothered about being handed the case. It was one that would involve every politician, business-owner, Freemason and journalist the town and much of the rest of the county could throw at them. It was sure to be a stinking, bottomless cesspit of self-interest and back-stabbing as every last one of them fought tooth and nail to benefit from Graball's unfortunate demise. Never mind there'd been a murder. That was quickly going to take a back seat. They'd soon find themselves under pressure to wrap up the case pronto, even if it risked letting the true killer get away scot-free. And if they upset anyone along the way, well they'd better have their tin hats with them, 'cause the amount of crap that would be dropped on them from a great height didn't bare thinking about.

"And what's your problem with that, sir?" asked a grinning Shapes, as they pulled up in front of the Conservative Club. "I thought you were going to tell me something bad. Politicians. Ugly old gits with too much money. It's perfect."

"I wonder about you sometimes, Shapes," replied Dykeman, opening the car door with a good deal of reluctance.

A small crowd of shoppers had gathered on the street, kept at a discreet distance from the club entrance by a uniformed PC. Eyes watched the two new arrivals with an eager expectation. Quite how word had got round so far, so soon no one was sure. But the grapevine had it down as a racing certainty there had been a mass murder inside the Conservative Club. Blood everywhere, someone had said. Another had added that his brother had a friend whose mother's neighbour's cousin worked in the kitchen there. Said he'd seen blood all over the curtains in the function room. Dripping off, it was. As the minutes had passed since the crowd began to form, so the body count had climbed. It was now up to at least half-a-dozen, and that wasn't including the injured.

THE CLUB OF DEATH

As Dykeman and Shapes approached the steps to the club, a tall, fresh-faced man with a thick black mop of hair falling over his eyes, launched himself out of the crowd.

"Inspector, it's Reynolds from the Oxford Observer. What can you tell us about the mass murder inside? We hear there could be six bodies. Is it true? When will..."

Shapes had the excited reporter by the throat before the man could get another word out. The journalist did a light-footed dance, his feet barely touching the ground, as the wild-eyed sergeant marched him backwards until he was pressed hard up against the front wall of the club.

"There'll be a press conference later, Reynolds from the Oxford Observer," snarled Shapes, the smell of beer washing over the younger man's face. "And until then, bugger off."

As the reporter scrabbled around on the ground, retrieving his notepad and pencil, the two officers strolled up the steps and in through the entrance. An impressed murmur rippled through the open-mouthed crowd.

Without much of a to-do, the two policemen were shown through to the function room by a member of staff who, thought Shapes, might be in need of a change of underwear; his white-washed face betraying familiar signs of shock. It promised much as to what they would find once they were introduced to the deceased. Blood and gore seemed highly likely, always an added bonus as far as he was concerned, since he always found it fascinating seeing examples of what people were capable of doing to another human being. On such occasions the whole idea of civilisation seemed to hang by a thread.

The function room had, they discovered upon entering, been turned into an impromptu holding pen for all the party-goers and members of staff on duty at the time. They were huddled in small groups around tables, noted Dykeman, near silent and looking deeply ill at ease. Excellent, both to have them already corralled and to see them in a docile mood. Half-empty glasses and partially-eaten puddings littered the tables. Abandoned trolleys, loaded with food, dishes and cutlery, loitered at the near end of the room. It all looked like the kind of sedate, sleep-inducing affair he would have expected in such a place. The sort of bash he was only too happy not to get invited to attend.

"Well done, Dartington," said Dykeman to the sole constable on duty in the room. "Impressed to see you've got everyone herded in here."

"Thank you, sir."

"What's the form then? Some sort of party, I hear?"

"Yes, sir. Party for the deceased, one Henry Graball. Celebrating a business anniversary, I'm told."

"And what happened?"

PC Dartington flipped open his notebook and started to peruse its contents as he replied. "Mr Graball has been murdered, sir. Stabbed several times in the neck and chest. Seems to have occurred between approximately 14.25 and 14.45. His wife is sitting over there, being comforted by some friends. The pathologist, Dr Delph, is already with the body, sir."

"Look at 'em, sir," grumbled Shapes. "They're all here. The mayor. The previous mayor and the one before that. And every businessman in the county worth anything must be in this room."

"Yes, I reckon you're right there, Shapes. We'll start upsetting them later. Where's the body, Dartington?"

"It's back down the stairs, sir. There's an office on the right when you get to the bottom. PC Trowel is in there with Dr Delph. Lots of blood. Nasty business," added Dartington, with a little wrinkle of the nose.

"Right. Keep this lot in here. Shapes and I will be back once we've taken a look at the body. Oh, who found it, the body?"

"Member of staff, sir. Saw the office door open and looked in. Reckon he wishes he hadn't."

SHEILA DELPH WAS A familiar and welcome face to Dykeman, who felt his heart rate tick up a notch or two as he set eyes on the middle-aged pathologist. Even murders had their upside.

"Hello Leslie," smiled the dark-haired woman crouching down by the corpse in the middle of the room. "Couldn't they send a proper policeman this time?"

She smiled at Dykeman, a winning little number that left him momentarily off-balance.

"Nice to see you too, Sheila. And I blame Shapes. He keeps telling the Chief Inspector he likes working on these bloodthirsty cases. Says it gets him all excited."

"The problem with that statement is I can believe it entirely. Hello Shapes."

"Ma'am," replied Shapes, already casting an eye round the room in the hope of spotting a clue or two.

"I suppose you'd like to know the cause of death?" asked Delph as she stood back up.

"It could come in handy," smiled Dykeman, joining his friend next to the corpse.

"He was stabbed. Once in the neck and at least five times in the chest. It's quite likely the wound to the neck would have led to death even without the other wounds. I would suspect it is the wound to the neck that has resulted in all this," added the pathologist, gesturing at the considerable amount of blood around the body.

"Yes, it's made a right old mess."

Dykeman took in the full extent of said mess. There seemed to be blood on just about everything within a two foot radius of the body. Carpet, chairs, desk and whatever was on the desk, it all now had at the least a fine spray of red. Some people, he thought, might even go so far as to describe it as art, of a sort.

"It would appear they cut an artery," observed the doctor, noting the somewhat astonished look on Dykeman's face.

"Happened to one of my dogs once, that did," chipped in Shapes.

"What did?" asked the inspector.

"Cut an artery. Did it on some broken glass. Was stone dead before the vet showed up. Bloody mess all over my lawn, there was."

"You make it sound like the dog did it on purpose, Shapes," suggested Dykeman.

"Wouldn't have put it past him."

His point made, Shapes spotted a supply of food on a tray that had been left on top of a filing cabinet. He closed on it without further ado.

"Angel cakes," smiled Shapes. "My favourites."

He helped himself to one of the tempting treats, then decided on two.

"Any cake is your favourite," replied Dykeman.

"That's not true, sir. I've never liked bread pudding."

"That's a pudding, not a cake."

"Cake where I grew up."

With a raised eyebrow, Dykeman turned back to Delph.

"Sorry about that. He gets worse all the time."

"I'm used to it now."

"Anything else you can tell me?"

"No, not now. I'll send you my report when I've had chance to take a close look later. There's a mild smell of alcohol in his mouth, but I wouldn't say he's had a great deal. And it doesn't look to me like he had a chance to defend himself. There's no sign of skin under his fingernails or bruising to the arms or hands. But all that's nothing more than my initial impressions. I won't let you hold me to it."

"Fair enough."

Dykeman walked once around the body, observing the blood-soaked clothing. A tailor-made suit, no doubt from an establishment in Oxford. Anything from a Banbury supplier was unlikely to be good enough for someone like Graball. The shoes, too, looked hand-made and expensive. His circuit completed, Dykeman squatted down low and pulled a pencil from a pocket, which he used to lever open Graball's jacket. The wallet was still there, poking out of an inside pocket. Dykeman eased it out and took a cursory look through its contents. It didn't really matter what was inside, rather the fact it was still there, suggesting very much this wasn't a crime motivated by theft.

"They didn't run off with his money, then," noted Delph.

"No. Not his watch either. I'd bet that's worth a few bob," added Dykeman, using the pencil to push back the cuff at Graball's left wrist.

He knew of Henry Graball, of course. It was hard to imagine there was anyone in the county who hadn't heard of the man. He'd appeared in the newspapers more often than Dykeman had. The inspector had heard him mentioned by the Chief Inspector, too, on more than one occasion. But he'd never encountered Graball, not until now, which wasn't exactly the ideal way to get to know someone. Wherever there was lots of money involved, as there obviously was this time, there was sure to be no shortage of suspects and, with several dozen people on the premises, it was going to be some challenge sorting the wheat from the chaff. This wasn't likely, mused Dykeman, to be a case they'd solve in a hurry.

Dykeman checked the remaining pockets in Graball's jacket and then the trousers. There was nothing of note, apart from a single sheet of paper, on which was written a brief message, saying that a David Rawlings needed to speak to him at once.

"Looks like this might be what brought him out here," said Dykeman, handing the note to Shapes, who read its contents, then slipped it into a pocket of his own.

"Want me to find out who this David Rawlings is, sir?"

"You'd better. Though I notice the phone is on the hook. Was it like that when you arrived?" asked the Inspector of Dr Delph.

"It was. But I also understand that Mr Graball was supposed to take the call in another room, not this one."

"Better add that to your list, Shapes."

"Sir."

"See anything else?" Dykeman asked his sergeant.

"Nothing. Shame the carpet is dark. Might have been in with a chance of some footprints if it was a lighter colour."

"What about the weapon?" enquired Dykeman, turning back to Delph, more in hope than expectation, since there was no sign of any weapon.

"Not here when I arrived. I would imagine there are a great many knives on the premises when there are so many people to cater for. Good luck with that one."

"Let's hope they didn't have time to dispose of it properly."

"Or clean it up," added Shapes.

"Yes, that too."

Dykeman was by now back on his feet. He spent a few moments contemplating, attempting to piece together possible scenarios. If the killer had been someone unknown to Graball, intent on launching a surprise attack on him before the man could either defend himself or raise the alarm, then they would have had to cover roughly twenty feet from the doorway in order to do so. That was a tall order and seemed unlikely, unless Graball had been distracted.

On the other hand, someone known to Graball would have been able to get right up close before making their strike. They'd need to hold their nerve of course, which he knew from his time working on many such cases, was easier said than done for all but the most cold-blooded of murderers. But such an assailant would have a marked advantage and likely leave the tycoon with little opportunity to put up a fight, especially if the first wound had been the one to the neck.

Then there was the escape. Surely it was just pure luck they were able to flee unnoticed? With so many people in the building, it would hardly have been a surprise if the assailant had encountered someone on their way out of the room. But even then, if they kept their cool, they might have been able to continue on their way without arousing suspicion. Something to look into.

"Right, we'd better get on with interviewing people," announced Dykeman, rubbing his hands together.

"There's a lot of the bleeders," replied Shapes, pleased with his pun.

"There are. I suggest divide and conquer is the way to go." Dykeman ignored his sergeant's attempt at humour, least he encourage the man. "Let's me and you, Shapes, interview the bloke who found Graball, then Graball's wife, assuming she's up to it. We might as well speak to anyone sitting at their table as well. The uniformed brigade can speak to the rest of 'em. How many constables have we got?"

"Six, sir."

"They've got a busy afternoon ahead of them," observed Dykeman, before turning to Dr Delph. "I'll have that report as soon as you're ready, Sheila, if you don't mind."

"Of course, Leslie. I wouldn't expect it to be any other way."

Chapter Three

Dykeman and Shapes set up shop in the office of the club manager, a nondescript man who, to the minds of both officers, seemed to blend into the wallpaper whenever he wasn't speaking. It was, they felt, an unnerving talent for someone to possess.

The office was a spacious room at the front of the building, with a large window looking out over the street, which meant they felt it necessary to close the blind in order to keep out prying eyes. It was clean and tidy to the point of obsession, thought Dykeman. There were four solid chairs and a large oak desk, behind which the Inspector parked himself as they waited for their first witness to arrive.

Shapes, sat on a chair to Dykeman's right, checked his watch and wrote down the time on his notepad, before stretching his fingers, then licking the tip of his pencil. Why he did that, he didn't know, since the taste was horrible, but he'd seen it done so many times in films it felt like the right thing to do, so he did.

Jack Browning, a short, thin man, who looked like he should have retired long ago, entered the room with a reluctant step, observed Dykeman. His bald head had a damp sheen to it and he glanced with nervous eyes at the intimidating presence of Shapes. There was, of course, nothing new in that, since most sane people found Shapes a disconcerting presence at the best of times. Dartington steered the witness to the allotted chair, then backed into a corner, so as to remain out of the way.

"Name?" demanded Dykeman.

"Jack Browning, sir."

"You're on the staff at the club?"

"I am, sir. One of the stewards."

"And how long have you been working here?"

"Eight years, sir."

"I'm told it was you who found the body of Henry Graball. Is that right?"

"Yes, sir. In the accountant's office."

"That's the room at the bottom of the stairs?"

"Yes, sir."

"Why did you go into the room?"

"The door was open, sir. It's supposed to be closed, when it's not being used."

"Tell me what you saw when you went into the room. Take your time. Every little detail you can remember will be helpful."

"Well," Browning stopped almost as soon as he'd started, looking into the air between himself and Dykeman. After a short while he resumed. "I almost didn't bother going in. Was only going to shut the door. But the light was on, see, so I opened the door and went inside. That's when I saw it, the body. He was lying there on the floor. Blood all over the place.

Nasty mess, it was. Hadn't seen anything like it since the war. I went over to him, Mr Graball, that is, and tried to find his pulse. He was dead as a dodo."

"What did you do then?"

"Called for you lot, sir."

"Was that using the phone in the accountant's room?"

"Yes, sir, it was."

"Was the phone already on the hook?"

"Yes, it was."

"You're sure of that?"

"I am that, sir."

Dykeman pulled a pencil from one of his jacket pockets, without at first being aware of what he was doing. It was, in fact, something he did often when he was questioning people and wanted a moment to decide on his next question or to unpick what he'd already been told. In this instance, the witness he'd at first thought might be too nervous to provide clear-headed answers to his questions, now appeared to be someone whose information they could rely on. It was odds on not all the witnesses would be half so level-headed and helpful. It was, therefore, worth his while asking further questions.

"Did you see anyone else entering or leaving the room?"

"No, none."

"You're sure?"

"I am that, sir."

Dykeman watched Shapes for a moment, his sergeant scribbling away in his usual cack-handed manner. It was a writing style all of his own and one he'd stuck to, despite several attempts by others to change it to something more comprehensible.

"Did you know the deceased?"

"Mr Graball, sir? Well, everyone knows him, don't they? I mean, we've all heard of him."

"But had you ever had any dealings with him before today?"

"No, sir. Seen him plenty of times, here at the club. Served him his food a few times too. But I've never been on proper speaking terms, as it were. Can't see a man like Mr Graball having much to do with the likes of me."

"Would you say Henry Graball was a popular man here at the Conservative Club?"

Browning moved in his chair for the first time since he'd sat down, noted Dykeman. A sign, perhaps, that the man was either about to tell a lie or was, at the very least, feeling uncomfortable about answering the question. Finally, thought Dykeman, he'd managed to home in on something that might prove useful.

"Well, it's not my place to go speaking about such things, sir. I don't rightly know what other people think about Mr Graball."

"But I get the impression it would be fair to say that he was not universally popular?"

"Well, like I say, sir, it's not my business..."

Dykeman brought a hand down hard and fast on the desk top and pressed home his attack, his voice raised, "Well, I'm making it your business. This is a murder investigation, not an afternoon picnic. Did Henry Graball have enemies, that's what I need to know."

Dykeman was pleased to notice that Browning had shrunk into his chair, his shoulders hunched. His mouth opened, closed, then opened again.

"He wasn't much liked by anyone, sir, if you ask me. All you ever heard was how greedy and mean he was."

"So, the man had enemies?"

"Well, I suppose so, sir."

"Any in particular?"

"Not that I know. Like I said, sir, Mr Graball didn't have anything to do with the likes of me."

Dykeman subsided back into his chair, a thin smile on his ever-so-slightly chubby face. That was better. It was a small beginning, but it was a beginning all the same. As he had suspected at the outset, Henry Graball had not, it seemed, got to the top of the pile without upsetting a few people along the way.

DAPHNE GRABALL PRESENTED an altogether different prospect for Dykeman. For one thing, the woman was understandably upset. Extremely so. This would need to be nothing more than a preliminary interview. A more in-depth one would have to wait until later, once she'd had time to regain some semblance of composure.

Dykeman couldn't help feeling genuinely sorry for the woman sitting opposite him, her face reddened by a flood of tears and her make-up smeared in every direction. She both looked and sounded distraught. Indeed, she appeared to be so upset that he had considered leaving even a brief conversation until later, but that would have risked setting back their investigation; something he wasn't keen on. It was entirely possible she had information that was vital to the case and he was concerned they should unearth it now, rather than risk any delay to their progress.

"I'm sorry that we need to speak to you now at all, Mrs Graball, but it would be an immense help if you could just answer a few standard questions. We can speak at greater length later."

She looked up at him from her slumped position and nodded her head so faintly Dykeman almost didn't notice the acknowledgement.

"I understand."

Her words were choked, struggling to get out of her mouth. She blew her nose on the tissue she held in one hand. As if realising his cue, Shapes stepped forward with a waste paper basket in one hand and a box of tissues in the other. Impressive, thought Dykeman, unaccustomed to such displays of understanding and consideration from his surly sergeant. It was fortunate the box of tissues had been sitting there on the desk, otherwise, Dykeman feared, Daphne Graball might have been presented with Shapes's infamously ancient and grey handkerchief.

"Excellent," said Dykeman, attempting a modestly upbeat note. "Had your husband received any threats to his life?"

Daphne Graball shook her head, then blew her nose again. Expensive watch she was wearing, noted Dykeman, as the sleeve of her blouse slipped a little way down her arm. The earrings too looked like they cost a few bob. Diamonds, if he wasn't mistaken, and he was certain he wasn't. Had Henry Graball wanted to show off his wife at his party, or was it her choice to flaunt some of their wealth? Did it make any difference? Dykeman thought it probably did not, but was reluctant to jump to any conclusions, especially at such an early stage in the case.

Shapes had sat back down and was looking eager, poised with his pencil and notepad, no look of annoyance or contempt on his leathery face. The old git must be going soft. Dykeman struggled to recall the last time his sergeant had shown such consideration. He failed in the attempt. Anyway, best get back to business.

"No phone calls or letters that left him... agitated?"

Again a shake of the head. The new widow straightened her back a little, bringing her head up so she could look Dykeman properly in the eye. A lone tear trickled down her right cheek. She dabbed at it with a fresh tissue.

"And no callers at the house who might have upset your husband?"

"No, Inspector, I'm afraid not."

"It's a rough game is business. I've seen plenty of examples of that over the years. Would it be fair to say your husband might have made a few enemies in his time? People who might have lost out to him and carried a grudge, that sort of thing?"

"I suppose so, but I never really have anything to do with Henry's business affairs."

Dykeman leaned forward a little, over the vast desk. Daphne Graball was getting her voice back and, with it, some of her composure. Dare he press on with a few more questions than he'd thought he would get away with before she collapsed into a sobbing heap? One or two, maybe, but he really didn't want to cause her any further upset. Her day had been bad enough already. A little more gentle probing, then he would leave her alone.

"Did your husband say why he was stepping out of the room? Any sign of who might have called him away?"

"A waiter brought him a note. Henry said he needed to take a phone call."

"Did he say who the phone call was from?"

"No, he didn't, I'm afraid. He wouldn't tell me who it was if it was about business. I used to enquire, when we were first married, but I stopped doing that a long time ago, when I realised Henry preferred to keep such things to himself."

"You didn't expect him to be gone long?"

"That's right. It was his day and he was so very much enjoying himself."

Daphne Graball began to weep again, the renewed thought of the pleasure her husband had been enjoying was too much for her.

Dykeman reconsidered his options. There didn't seem to be anything much to gain by pushing on with more questions, not yet. Mrs Graball had held it together well enough up to now, but was obviously still very upset. Best they be grateful for what they'd got out of her so far and put off further questioning until later. There was also the small matter of the Chief Inspector, who would not be amused if reports got back to him suggesting his two officers had given offence to the new widow.

"Well, that will be all for now, Mrs Graball. We'll speak again another time but if you do think of anything in the meantime you feel I ought to know, then you can call Shapes or myself any time you like."

"Thank you, Inspector."

As the door closed behind the tearful Daphne Graball and Phillip Underwood, who had been waiting outside the room escort her back to the function room, Dykeman turned towards Shapes.

"Well, what do you think?"

"What, about her?" There was a short pause. "You don't reckon she had anything to do with it?"

Shapes looked, noted Dykeman, positively astonished. The Inspector nearly laughed.

"Got to consider all the options. Hardly unknown for a wife to bump off a rich husband."

"Bugger off, she didn't do it...."

"Going soft in your old age, Shapes?"

"Sod off... sir"

WITH A SHORT HALT TO proceedings having been declared by his boss, who needed to take a tinkle, Shapes had wandered off in search of grub and a nice, fresh cup of tea. Why he should have to go looking for these things when the building was stuffed full of waiters and waitresses was another matter. Useless bunch of layabouts. He'd give 'em a piece of his mind when he tracked one of them down.

As he walked along the long narrow corridor away from their temporary base, he thought again about the new widow. Daphne Graball reminded him of a teacher he'd had at primary school. She'd taught his class for two years when he was nine and ten. A patient, helpful woman, it was the first and, as it turned out, only time he'd had a teacher who gave him any real enthusiasm for learning, as opposed to playing football and trying to steal chocolate bars from the nearby corner shop.

Every other teacher during his school days had ruled the class-room like they were on special release from the nearest army base, barking out orders, handing out punishment with rulers and canes like they were on some kind of bonus for doing so. None of 'em did anything to make school a happy experience, as far as he was concerned.

The funny thing was, the nice teacher had no problems with the kids' behaviour, even though she never once swore at them or gave anyone a whack over the knuckles. Of course, he'd realised once he'd become a grown-up that they all behaved themselves because they respected her. What was her name? Mrs French, that was it. No first name. The school treated staff first names like they were some kind of state secret.

Yes, there was something of the Mrs French about Daphne Graball. Nice didn't do either of them justice, but the word kept popping into his head all the same. There ought to be more people in the world like Mrs French. It would be a much better place for it.

And since he couldn't see Mrs French as a cold-blooded killer, Shapes also couldn't see Daphne Graball as one. It should have bothered him, that he knew, but he didn't care. As far as he was concerned, she was innocent as a newborn baby. Most likely, Dykeman hadn't made his mind up about her yet, but he'd see sense. She had enough on her plate right now, without having to deal with being accused of her old man's murder.

He reached the bottom of the stairs in the hallway, having seen hide nor hair of anyone else, then stopped, deep in thought, unaware that he was scratching his backside.

What a nasty business this murder was. Blood everywhere. You had to wonder how the killer got away without getting any of the blood on their own clothes. Didn't seem likely they'd be able to manage that. In which case, if it was someone still on the premises, they'd either had to change into some fresh clothes or else run the risk of waltzing around the place with the red stuff still splashed all over them. There was a chance they could have covered up any blood stains on their clothes. If it was a fella, they could have taken their jacket off before doing the deed, then slipped it back on afterwards. Even so, they'd be taking a chance on someone noticing a drop or two of blood on their shirt. Seemed more likely they'd want to have a change of clothes to hand. An interesting thought.

"Sergeant Shapes, you look lost. Can I help?"

"Mr Underwood," Shapes brought himself back to the world to find the large figure of the club chairman he'd met earlier standing in front of him. "What are you doing out here, sir? Oughtn't you to be in the big room with all the others?"

He bloody well should, Shapes knew that already. Couldn't have witnesses - and possible killers, for that matter - wandering around the place. He straightened himself up in an effort to feel less intimidated by the chairman, who, like a lot of his sort, came across like he felt he owned the whole damned world.

"Had some trouble with one of the waiters. One of your constables asked me to sort things out. Nerves, poor fellow. Never seen a corpse before. I suppose you have, of course?"

"Plenty. Well, seeing as you're here, can you tell me where I can get a cup of tea for me and the Inspector? Can't find anyone around."

"No, you have pretty much all of them locked up with the rest of us. If you'd like to follow me, I'll take you to the kitchens myself. They're a deep, dark dungeon that I try to stay away from most of the time. Rumours do the rounds that people sometimes go in there and are never seen again."

Shapes chose to ignore Underwood's light-hearted conversation. For one thing, the sergeant didn't much care for people like the club chairman. To him they were arrogant toffs; people who looked down on the likes of him with an unjustified air of superiority. The man would probably start telling him next that he'd already worked out who the killer was.

They went through a set of double doors and set off down another stretch of corridor, this one poorly lit, at a pace Shapes struggled to keep up with.

"Of course, it won't be someone at Graball's party who killed him, you know," said the club chairman, glancing back over a shoulder.

Here we go, thought Shapes. He'll be telling me now it was a Communist, out to bash the capitalist establishment, or some nutter who'd wandered in off the street.

"What d'you mean?" he asked, playing dumb.

"The killer. They won't be someone from that room down there. I wouldn't say they're all best chums with poor old Henry - in fact a few of them are probably glad he's been done in - but none of them are capable of cold-blooded murder. Most of them wouldn't know how to kill a man and the others, well, a few wouldn't have the balls and the rest don't have any reason. No, if you ask me, it's either a member of the staff, God forbid, or someone who Henry must have offended in some other capacity. A spurned lover, perhaps, or... here we are, the kitchens."

Underwood took them through yet another set of double-doors, into a kitchen, the considerable size of which surprised the sergeant. Underwood saw the astonished look on the policeman's face.

"Sizeable place, what? Used to have functions here most weeks in the old days and lots of members would come in for luncheon. Not like that now, of course. Could really do with a smaller facility. Cheaper to run. Now then, let's see if there's anyone around who can sort out a pot of tea for you."

Underwood was about to set off in search of a member of staff, but Shapes had other thoughts.

"Hold on. What's that you said about a lover just now?"

"A lover? Did I really?"

Shapes could hardly avoid noticing the exaggerated smile on the club chairman's face. In fact, it was more like a chimp's grin. Something was afoot.

"You did and I reckon you weren't mucking about."

"You're so observant, Sergeant."

Idiot, thought Shapes, observant enough to know when he was having the mickey taken.

"So they say."

"Well, I suppose Henry's dead and soon to be buried, so it can't harm him, but you will be sensitive to Daphne's feelings, won't you?"

Interesting, thought Shapes, that Underwood switched so quickly to a serious tone as soon as he mentioned Daphne Graball.

"We've spoken to her already. Seems like a nice woman."

"She's an absolutely wonderful human being, sergeant, and I really wouldn't like her to be caused any more distress than she has already suffered. I trust I make myself clear?"

Phillip Underwood glared at Shapes in a manner that made the sergeant a little uncomfortable. There was, decided, Shapes more to this than met the eye. He made a mental note and filed it away for later.

"So, what d'you know about Henry Graball's extra-marital affairs?"

Shapes was quite pleased with the way he'd pitched the question. Sounded better than asking where the dead man had been getting his leg over.

"Well, one thing is for sure, Sergeant, Henry Graball was a man with an appetite, if I can put it like that. He didn't restrict himself to just the one mistress. I know of four and I shouldn't doubt there were many others. Henry got bored with them, sooner or later, especially if they started getting a little too clingy."

"Didn't his wife know what he was up to?"

"I'm not entirely certain, but I don't think so, no. Henry was discreet, most of the time. Always paid them off well. I suppose you could call it hush money. No, unless someone in the know mentioned it to her, I doubt Daphne was aware."

"Did he have somewhere he kept them? A flat, maybe?"

"I believe so, though if he did he never took me anywhere near the place. Think there's only so much a chap is prepared to share with his friends."

"Don't suppose you know any of their names?

"I met two young women with him over the years. A skinny, sour-faced red-head he brought along to a drinks reception in Oxford several years ago. Can't remember her name. Too long ago. She didn't seem like his type, to be honest. Always thought of Graball as a man with a taste for the larger woman, not bean-poles."

"You said there was another one you met?"

"Oh, yes. Wendy something-or-other. Met her a couple of times. Attractive young thing. Late twenties or early thirties, I'd say. Wouldn't mind taking her out for a drink myself, if I was a single man."

"Now's your chance," prompted Shapes. "What with Graball being off the scene."

Shapes studied the other man closely. In his experience, well-to-do old gits like Underwood often got more than their fair share of totty. They seemed to think it was a natural right. Was there, wondered Shapes, any chance the murder of Henry Graball was a straight-forward case of jealousy or some sort of scheme between the latest mistress and someone like Phillip Underwood to help themselves to a chunk of Henry Graball's fortune?

"Steady on, Sergeant. You don't want to go getting the wrong idea. Might end up wasting a lot of your time barking up the wrong tree."

"She here today, this Wendy what's-her-name?"

"Should damn well hope not," replied Underwood, his eyebrows reaching for the ceiling. "When Daphne's here too? Never does any good for a man to have his wife and his mistress in the same place at the same time. That would be asking for trouble, plain and simple."

"Been seeing her long then, had he?"

"I reckon he had, yes. That is long by his standards. Maybe... eighteen months, or something of the sort. That's just conjecture on my part, you understand."

"Fair enough."

"Mind you, he'd put an end to it. Just recently."

Shapes scratched a spot on the back of his neck, not realising he'd pulled away the small scab covering it. A small bobble of blood welled up. As he shifted his head, the blood smeared against his collar, leaving a deep-red stain.

"Just how recently would that be?"

"Well, Henry had been having some trouble with this one, as I understand it. Seems she wouldn't clear off when he told her to. We met up for drinks last Thursday lunchtime, here at the club. He'd given the woman the old heave-ho the day before, but turned out she had the idea Henry might leave Daphne and move in with her. Couldn't believe he'd had enough of her, or so he said. Find that part hard to believe, myself. One would be inclined to think it was the money she was afraid of missing out on, not Henry's body."

"Funny, the effect a lot of cash can have on a woman."

"Something Henry appreciated only too well."

"And you sure you can't remember her surname?"

"I honestly don't think Henry mentioned it. Ah, Florence, the very woman."

Underwood had noticed a small, elderly woman walking into the kitchen, carrying a tray of dirty cups.

"Oh, didn't expect to see you in here, Mr Underwood. Can I help?"

"You certainly can. Sergeant Shapes here is rather desperate for a cup of tea. Biscuits too, I shouldn't doubt."

The woman looked at Shapes, narrowed her eyes, then started to walk away as she replied. "Of course, Mr Underwood. But he'll have to take a tray away with him. I'm too busy to be running around, what with this murder and all. Everyone's wanting cups of tea right now."

Chapter Four

"Where you been with this, Shapes? Timbuktu and back? It's barely lukewarm."

Dykeman knocked back the rest of his tea in one go, then set about a digestive biscuit. Shapes bridled at the complaint. There he was, running around like some sort of personal servant for his lazy boss and finding out highly useful information along the way, and all Dykeman could do in return was whinge. He'd a mind to put something nasty in the next cup of tea he rustled up for him. The options on that front were practically limitless.

"It's a long way from the kitchen, sir."

Dykeman ignored the excuse. He was thinking about the news his sergeant had brought back with him. A heartlessly dumped mistress. One who hadn't taken the news any too well. There was a motive for sticking a knife into Graball, if ever there was one. Certainly the best they'd come up with so far.

"We'll need to track down this 'ere mistress. Should be right up your street, finding a sexy young woman."

"Thank you, sir."

Shapes's mood took a little upward tick. He began to wonder how many sexy young women he would have to interview along the way, until he eventually found the right one. All in a day's work and all that.

"Right, who's next for the spotlight?"

"It's the mayor, sir. Insists on having a word. Probably a waste of time, but he won't lay off until he's had his say."

"And who is the mayor this year? Can't recall having met this one yet."

"Nigel Nettle."

"Well, let's hope he doesn't sting."

Dykeman grinned, delighted at his own joke. Shapes remained stony-faced, disgusted at his boss' pathetic attempt at humour.

"You're not expecting me to laugh at that one, are you?"

"You're just jealous you didn't get in there first, Shapes."

"If you say so, sir."

"I do. Now then, wheel him in and let's see what he's got to say for himself."

The short, podgy man, with his round, wire-framed glasses and rapidly thinning hair, that Shapes escorted into the room reminded Dykeman of the former landlord at his local pub. The resemblance was so close they could almost have been twins. It was unnerving. It also gave the inspector a sudden taste for a decent pint of beer. It was tempting to have one fetched from the club bar, but that might not be good for appearances. Someone was sure to tip-off the Chief Inspector.

"Mr Nettle? Or am I supposed to call you Your Worship?" prompted Dykeman.

Nettle managed a brief chuckle before replying. "I prefer Your Lordship, if that's alright with you. No, no, only kidding. Nettle is fine."

Shapes shook his head and grimaced. Dykeman was glad his sergeant was not in the mayor's line of sight.

"Good. How long do you get to be mayor for? Must take up a lot of time, I would imagine."

"Pretty much a full-time job, yes. What with all those ribbons to be cut, school plays to be watched and the endless meetings. Yes, the meetings alone take up more hours than I care to count. But I agreed to it, so can't go complaining. And it's a real honour, goes without saying, to be the mayor. Yes, a real honour. It's a twelve month stint, then, so long as you've been well-behaved, they set you free. There's been a few who've served more than one term, but most of us only do the one year."

"And did you know Henry Graball before you became mayor?"

"Oh, yes. Known him for years. I used to run our family's haulage business, you see. Got a dozen lorries now, we have. Retired last year and still only fifty-eight. Remarkable, don't you think. Always imagined I'd be flogging away at it until the day I dropped down dead. My two sons run the business now. Shoved me aside, in the nicest way, you understand, and have made an excellent start to things. Want to double the number of lorries, they say. That's how I know, or knew, Henry. We transport a lot of the products from his engineering business on to his customers. He's been our main customer for, oh, must be something like ten years now. Bit of a worry that, come to think of it. Makes you wonder..."

Getting Nettle to talk clearly wasn't going to be a problem, decided Dykeman, who felt it necessary to cut off another digression and get them back to the matter at hand.

"And how would you describe Graball's style of doing business?"

Nettle smiled, then fiddled with his glasses.

"I suppose some people have been telling you that Henry was a nasty piece of work."

"There seems to be an impression of the sort out there."

"I always got on perfectly well with him. It's fair to say, he always drives a hard bargain. Wants the best for himself and his business. But, there again, who doesn't, eh? We all want the best deal we can get. And one thing I will say is that Henry always paid his bills on time. Never early, mind, but never, ever late. That's more than you can say for some."

Funny thing, the way the man was obviously trying to maintain a serious demeanour, yet he seemed unable to shake off a permanent look of amusement. He'd probably been born like that. One of life's smilers, always capable of seeing a silver lining in even the darkest of clouds, mused Dykeman. Must annoy his friends.

"Would you say he made any enemies along the way?"

"Inspector, we're talking about commerce here. We all upset people sooner or later. Can't be helped. Sometimes people get an idea into their head that things are what they're not. Tell themselves they've won a contract or made a sale that no one has actually signed up to. We've all been there. Yes, Henry's made a few enemies. He's put a few competitors out of business in his time. But that's the way of things. Survival of the fittest. I can tell you, the transport business is one of the worst. Cut-throat it is. Margins are wafer thin and some folk aren't shy of trying to bribe their way to winning a contract."

"So, there's no one particular, no one with reason to have a serious grudge against Graball?"

The mayor hesitated, his mouth opening but no words coming out. His nose twitched and he glanced down at the desk.

"Well, I wouldn't go so far as to say that, no. There are one or two who have taken exception to what Henry has done."

"And they would be?"

"Henry could be a ruthless piece of... work at times, Inspector. Not often. But if he felt the need and the opportunity was there, well, he was capable of pressing home an attack where others might not. Nothing illegal, you understand. Everything above board. But the sort of thing that could upset some people. There was an incident three or four years ago with the man who was mayor then, Matthew Louch. Had rather an unpleasant outcome for the poor chap. All of his own doing, needless to say. As it happens, he's here today, with his wife. You could ask him yourself."

Dykeman extracted the basics of the incident from Underwood, before moving on.

"We'll be doing that. That's very helpful, Mr Nettle. One final question. When did you last see Henry Graball, by which I mean the time?"

"Oh, well, that's a little hard to say. We were all sat round the top table, when one of the waiters brought him a note. He left to take a phone call. Afraid I didn't happen to notice the time. One of the others might have done. Have you tried asking them?"

"Not yet. Right, thank you for your time, Mr Nettle. Not often I get to question the town mayor about a murder."

"Not often I get to be anywhere near a murder, Inspector."

"MR LOUCH, PLEASE TAKE a seat."

Dykeman made the offer barely one second before Shapes shoved the chair into the back of Matthew Louch's legs, causing him to sit down with a little more force than he would have liked. Louch began to turn his head to complain, then decided against it. The sergeant, who'd marched him out of the function room, didn't look like the sort of policeman you should risk upsetting. There'd been stories going round town for years about the sort of interrogation tactics they used at the town's police station and he wasn't keen on finding out for himself whether or not they were true. Better to focus on the large man sitting behind the desk. He looked a little less threatening and was far enough away not to be able to reach him.

Louch loosened his tie and undid the button on the front of his jacket. He had begun to feel rather warm. Given his unwelcome and unpleasant run-in with the law three years earlier, finding himself once more under police scrutiny left him feeling rather uncomfortable. He hoped the interview would be brief. He also hoped whatever questions they threw at him weren't all that searching, since there were things he would prefer were not brought back into the public eye, especially given the current circumstances. That could prove rather awkward.

"Understand you were a friend of the deceased?" prompted Dykeman.

"Well, more of an acquaintance, I would say."

Louch brought his hands into his lap and began to fiddle with his fingers, a move that did not escape the eye of either policeman. Excellent, thought Dykeman, got the man a little off-balance already. He never did like his witnesses or potential suspects to feel too comfortable. Being a little ill at ease, he felt, made it harder for a person to fabric the truth, or avoid it, come to that. Odd accent, though. Almost local, but with a dash of, what was it? West Country, maybe. Well, we've all got our crosses to bear, mused the Inspector.

"An acquaintance, you say," repeated Dykeman, sounding as though he was less than convinced. "Some would say you were the worst of enemies, what do you say to that?"

"Well," Louch looked down at his hands. "We did have our differences, though to say we were the worst of enemies would be putting it a bit strong."

"You had your differences? Sergeant Shapes has a way with words, why don't we ask him what he thinks? How would you put it, Shapes?"

"I reckon Mr Louch must have hated Graball's guts. Would have happily shoved him under a bus, if he got half a chance, after what the deceased did to him, sir."

Dykeman remained silent, waiting for a response. Phillip Underwood's description of the events that had put an end to Louch's term as mayor suggested there had been no foul play on Graball's part, but he had played a rather prominent role in the former mayor's decision to resign, rather than see the press get hold of some rather incriminating information. That alone was plenty enough reason for Louch to hate Graball's guts. Dykeman had himself only the most vague recollection of the events at the time and, if truth be told, he wouldn't even have been able to recall the name of the doomed mayor.

Matthew Louch sat fully up-right and met the gaze of the Inspector full on.

"It's hardly surprising if I don't like the man, not after what he did to me." The words were spoken with some force.

Louch's face had, noticed Dykeman, taken on a sullen appearance. It was as if he couldn't make up his mind whether to be angry or depressed, so settled on frustration and mild petulance. Odd really. Under the circumstances, he might have been expected to blow a fuse. Perhaps a gentle prod would help. If not, a sharper one surely would.

"And just what did Banbury's greatest ever industrial titan do to you that was so bad?"

"He ruined me, that's what. He damn well ruined me. Threatened to go running to the press with some story about irregularities with election finances that I knew nothing at all about. I was the town mayor at the time and hoping to be selected as the constituency's next Conservative Party candidate for Parliament. Graball told me that if the story should find its way to the press, I'd be finished. The public would never believe I wasn't aware of what had been going on and, in any case, I should have known what was happening because the stupid fools who messed up were working for me. He smiled when he told me that I'd have to resign. Loved every second of it, he did. I claimed that I needed to resign due to a problem with my health, but rumours soon started spreading around the town, no doubt started by Graball, and, in no time at all, my political career had gone up in smoke."

"Mm, and why would Graball have wanted to do something like that?"

"Revenge. The council turned down a planning request of his. The thing was, it didn't mean he lost any money, just that he missed out on making a lot. But you know what," continued Louch, picking up the pace and sounding altogether more animated. "All we did was stick to Council policy. We didn't pick on him specially. Just treated him the same as everyone else."

There was a spark in his eyes now and, noticed Dykeman, a hint of venom. All was very definitely not forgiven nor forgotten.

"Maybe that was the problem. He didn't like being treated like everyone else."

"That's an understatement. He always thought he was better than the rest of us. His type always do."

"So, why are you here today? Would have thought you'd have nothing to do with Graball after what happened?"

"It was my wife, Sheila. She insisted we accept the invitation. I'd no doubt Graball just wanted to rub my nose in the dirt. He was like that. As nasty a piece of works as you'll ever find. But it's hard making a living in the professions without having good contacts and everyone who's anyone in the whole district is here today. Sheila was adamant we couldn't allow such an opportunity to pass by. So, here we are."

"Should have words with your wife. Looks like she's got you into a bit of a pickle. One with a nasty aftertaste."

"I don't think that would do any good, Inspector."

"And how do you feel about Graball getting topped?"

"Surprised someone hadn't done something of the sort sooner. He must have ruined lots of lives and made a lot of enemies."

Dykeman sat back in his chair and brought his fingers up in front of his chest, tapping them together. He had before him a genuine suspect, someone with a decent reason to stick a knife in Graball, several times over. But was he capable and did he get the opportunity? Shapes's eyes had narrowed and he held his pencil and notepad close together, as if keen not to miss a single word. It was an indication to Dykeman that Shapes believed they were on to something.

"Did you leave the room at any point after Graball went to talk on the phone?"

"Yes, for a couple of minutes, to go to the toilet."

"Anyone see you there, pointing Percy at the porcelain?"

There was a pause before Louch answered, a degree of resignation in his voice. "No, I don't believe there was anyone else there."

"So, we've only your word, it seems."

Dykeman made no attempt to disguise the element of accusation in his voice, after all, as far as he was concerned, he was looking at a man with both a motive and an opportunity for murder.

"But, hold on, I did see someone in the hallway."

"Really and who was that?"

"A member of the staff. A ratty-looking fellow. He'd been arguing with Graball and came storming down the corridor afterwards. I know he got a decent look at me."

"And what had they been arguing about, do you know?"

"Couldn't hear, I'm afraid. Too far away. Just happened to notice they were both quite animated. I suspect they heard me coming and that put an end to their discussion. But the man definitely got a good look at me."

Matthew Louch was relieved to have informed them of his encounter with this unnamed member of the staff. Shame it didn't do him a whole lot of good in terms of an alibi, but the part about the argument between Graball and the mystery man appeared to be of interest to the Inspector.

"That should mean we can place you in the corridor, Mr Louch. Of course, it doesn't mean you didn't track down Henry Graball after that."

Louch's shoulders slumped and the flicker of hope that had appeared on his face disappeared.

"Suppose that makes me a suspect, does it?"

"You'd have to agree, Mr Louch, that you've got a motive and, unless we can find someone to say otherwise, you had the opportunity. So, yes, that would make you a suspect."

Dykeman noticed that Shapes's hand was positively dancing across the paper as he wrote those last few words down. He always liked a nice early breakthrough in a case, did his sergeant, though Dykeman himself felt there was a good way to go yet before they could start thinking about charging anyone.

"WELL, WELL, WELL, THAT was an interesting one," announced Shapes, having returned to the office after taking Louch back to the function room.

"It was indeed," replied Dykeman He was busy munching on a biscuit, keen to get his share before Shapes swooped and woofed down the lot. "What do you think, then? Reckon he might have done it?"

"Bloody good reason to. Graball ruined him. Why not get your own back by sticking a knife in the man? Don't know though. Didn't look to me like he'd have the nerve. I reckon he's a bit of a softie."

"Remember, he's an accountant. Probably a ruthless wolf hiding under that sheep's clothing. And we haven't met his wife yet. Sounds like she might be the pushy sort. That can be enough to drive the best of men round the bend. But you're right, we shouldn't go jumping to conclusions."

"You have noticed how many people are out there that we're going to have to speak to. Even with half a dozen officers, I reckon we're going to be here all day. And they'll start grumbling soon. Too hot, too cold, hungry, bored, jobs to do. Bla, bla, bla."

"Tough, I don't want any of them leaving until we've spoken to the lot. Don't care how well they know the Chief Inspector either. We're going to have to do some serious digging, what with there being so many people involved and, who knows, half of them might have a good reason for holding a grudge against Graball."

"I reckon his wife is the most likely. She'd probably had enough of him, what with the mistresses and him spending all his time at work. Decided to trade him in for a new bloke," said Shapes, perusing the shrinking supply of biscuits. It was a worrying state of affairs, so he grabbed half-a-dozen digestives.

Dykeman stood up. He was, all of a sudden, restless, keen to see what was going on elsewhere. Perhaps they were missing out on something important and that wouldn't do, not with him being in charge and all.

"Come on, let's see how they're getting on in the function room. I've had enough of being cooped up in here."

THE NEWS WAS BETTER than Dykeman had been expecting, although he didn't know why he had any reason to think otherwise. The constables assigned to the task had made good progress and were confident they would get through the whole assembled mass before it grew dark. That put his mind at ease, since, despite his show of bravado to Shapes, he knew full well there were plenty of people in the room capable of pulling strings back at police headquarters. The last thing he wanted was any of them clearing off home before being interviewed.

He and Shapes were perusing some of the notes made thus far when Matthew Louch approached them, accompanied by a slender, dark-haired woman, who caught Dykeman's eye with a gentle and very feminine smile. It gave him a bit of a flutter.

"Inspector Dykeman, this is my wife, Sheila," announced Matthew Louch, before adding, "Darling, this is Inspector Dykeman. He's heading up the murder investigation."

It didn't escape the attention of Sergeant Shapes that he was excluded from the pleasantries. That was a black mark for Matthew Louch.

"Inspector, delighted to meet you. Matthew tells me that you gave him quite the grilling. It does sound as though we have the right man on the case. So good to know we have someone capable tracking down this fiend."

Dykeman wasn't entirely sure the compliment was genuine, but the woman's soft voice and deep green eyes were tempting enough for him to give her the benefit of the doubt with little hesitation.

"Don't you worry, Mrs Louch, we'll get our man. We always do, eh Shapes."

"Sir," confirmed Shapes, wondering what the woman was after.

"You'll understand if I am a little lacking in sympathy for the recently departed, Inspector," continued Sheila Louch. "But I do feel so awfully sorry for poor Daphne. She really is a wonderful woman and it's terrible to see her being put through such an ordeal. You will treat her kindly, won't you?"

"Always a difficult part of any murder case, is dealing with the bereaved spouse. Though it's sad to have to say so, Shapes and I have had a fair amount of practice at it over the years. Never gets any easier, mind. Have to say, Mrs Graball has been holding up impressively well. At least she's amongst friends here."

"Yes, she certainly is," replied Sheila Louch, taking hold of her husband's arm. "We do understand why you might think Matthew had a reason to murder Henry Graball, Inspector, but I wanted to assure you, Matthew's really not the kind of man who could do such a thing. He just doesn't have it in him."

There was a look of anguish on her face as she spoke and she pulled herself closer to her husband. It was an appeal that was capable of chipping away at the stoniest of foundations and Dykeman felt a little tremble within. Lucky fellow, was Matthew Louch.

"Well, we're counting no chickens here, Mrs Louch, I can assure you of that. But until we've been able to rule out an individual they remain a suspect and that goes for every single person in this room."

Dykeman puffed himself up just a tad as he spoke, feeling the need to stand tall and strong.

"Me too, Inspector?"

"Yes, you too, Mrs Louch."

"Well, I do hope you find whoever is responsible very soon, then the rest of us can rest easy."

As the Louches walked away, Shapes scratched behind his right ear and raised an eyebrow.

"She seems too good a catch for him," he observed, studying the gentle lift and fall of her hips.

"Mm," was all Dykeman could manage by way of a reply, his mind already deep in thought.

THEY HAD BARELY SET foot back inside the police station when a summons came for Dykeman to head upstairs and provide the Chief Inspector with a full and detailed update on progress. Shapes had provided moral support by laughing at his superior, before strolling off in the direction of the canteen, whistling as he went.

It was twenty minutes before Dykeman re-joined his sergeant, now on to his second cup of tea and almost through the latest edition of the Racing Herald.

"I told you Nancy's Fancy was worth backing," he announced as Dykeman parked himself on the chair opposite him. "Won by three lengths at Aintree yesterday. Missed out on a few bob there, we did."

"Wants the case all wrapped up by the end of tomorrow, he does," growled Dykeman, ignoring Shapes's observations on the previous day's racing. "Worried about the bad publicity for the town, he says. Got nothing at all to do with the possible bad publicity for himself," added the irritated Inspector.

"Yeah, I'll bet. Stupid old git's forgotten what it's like being a real copper. Been too long since he did any proper policing."

"Don't think there's anyone here who's ever seen him actually working on a case. Does make you wonder," Dykeman said, giving his tea another stir. "I tried telling him there's flipping hundreds of statements to take but he wasn't having it. Says since we have half his constables working on the case, we ought be able to crack on through it in no time. Spot the glaring omissions, he said, then fall on the guilty party like a swooping falcon. Nothing to it."

"Tell you how to tie your shoe laces as well, did he?"

"Might as well have done, for all the difference it would have made."

Dykeman sipped at his tea. It was too hot. That was another thing that annoyed him.

"What next then, sir?"

"We ought to get a look at Graball's will, see who gets all the loot. Never know, there might be something unexpected in there. Something that helps point us towards another suspect."

"Secret family, that sort of thing? Links to the North Oxfordshire Morris Dancers?"

Shapes leaned back and stretched. He liked the station canteen; it often felt more inviting than his own place, which lacked a woman's touch.

"What's up with you? Been drinking?"

"Not yet, bit too early."

"Then why are you so happy all of a sudden?"

"We've not had a decent case in ages. About bloody time something juicy came along and we've got a right little number here. Makes it all worth getting out of bed for in the morning."

"Ok, Mr Happy, what do you think of things so far? Who are your most likely candidates?"

"Blimey, there's dozens of 'em. Matthew Louch, he's one. Best motive we've found so far."

"The widow, what about her?"

"Don't know. Maybe not. Don't seem the type to me."

"What if she found out about Graball's mistresses? Maybe someone tipped her off."

Shapes picked at a bit of biscuit that had lodged between two teeth.

"Go on then, her too. But my money's on someone else. Most likely someone he's put out of business."

"So, it's revenge, is it?"

"That's the little puppy."

"Well, like I've said before, every murder there's ever been is down to either sex, money or revenge and this one will be no different. This tea's too hot. Come on, let's see if we can track down Graball's solicitor."

"You'll be lucky, sir. They've probably packed up for the day by now. Bunch of lazy, work-shy blood-suckers, they are."

Chapter Five

The following morning, after several hours spent pouring over interview statements with two of the constables, it was close on eleven o'clock by the time Shapes returned to the small office he shared with Dykeman. The Inspector was sitting behind his desk, singing to himself. Shapes was long since used to Dykeman's dire attempts at singing, but, even by his normal standards, this effort was bad.

"Cole Porter, sir?"

"It is. Didn't think you liked the maestro's music, Shapes?"

"I don't, but can't help recognising it; not when you're singing it so much of the time."

"Excellent, glad to hear all my efforts haven't been going to waste."

"I said I recognised it. Didn't say I liked it."

"One step at a time, Shapes. We'll have you singing it in the bath sooner or later."

"Anyway, what's got you sounding so happy?"

"I'm always happy, Shapes. The very definition of a happy man, that's me."

"If you say so, sir."

"I do, although it's fair to say I am extra-special happy right now. There's been a development."

"Would that be with the case, sir, or your cabbage patch?"

"My cabbages are looking wonderful, Shapes. Not a caterpillar any where near 'em."

Shapes had realised by now that Dykeman was in the right kind of upbeat mood to string him along. It was the kind of thing that amused his boss. The best way to respond was to ignore it and resist rising to the bait. There was a period of silence, during which Dykeman twiddled his pencil and Shapes's nose twitched. Shapes felt himself getting annoyed, but knew he shouldn't let on, because doing that would mean Dykeman had won a cheap victory, of sorts.

"So," began Shapes, cutting across the silence. "I'm betting either someone has owned up. Either that, or every last one of the guests at the party has dropped down dead. Food poisoning. That would make things a bit awkward."

"Cynicism, Shapes? It doesn't become you."

The smirk on Dykeman's face needed wiping off, ideally with a sledgehammer, decided Shapes. Sadly, there wasn't one to hand.

"Everyone's a cynic, sir. That's what happens to you when you stop being a kid."

"Dartington has made a discovery."

At last, thought Shapes. Dykeman could be seriously annoying at times.

"What's that, then? Got nits, has he? I told him to get his hair cut."

Dykeman smiled, then placed his pencil on the desk.

"There was someone amongst the guests at the Conservative Club who wasn't on the invitation list and neither were they staff."

Now, that is interesting, thought Shapes. It was clear from the tone of Dykeman's voice that this, as yet, unnamed individual had at once gone to the top of their list of priorities. One very particular possibility presented itself to the curious sergeant.

"A woman, was it, sir?"

"It certainly was."

"You don't suppose?"

"Got my fingers and my toes crossed, Shapes." Dykeman's smile broadened. "A dumped mistress with a temper could be just the sort to stick a knife into her former lover's podgy body."

Dykeman was still grinning as they marched into the station car park in search of a vehicle they could use for the drive south to Oxford, where they would find their latest suspect.

THE MORRIS MINOR THEY'D found loitering in the car park had developed an unhealthy high-pitched whine by the time they reached Oxford. Dykeman had shoved his fingers in his ears for the last five miles, but Shapes, who was driving, didn't have the benefit of such a luxury. As a result, by the time they pulled into the car park of the Oxford City police headquarters, Shapes had acquired a solid headache and a bad mood to match.

"Best leave this thing here, Shapes. When we're done, we'll take the train back to Banbury."

Dykeman took the muffled mutterings coming from the driver's seat as agreement.

The flat that was home to Wendy Slip was a fifteen-minute walk east from the city centre. The two policemen were familiar with the centre of Oxford, having made many a visit, but that didn't stop at least one of them from admiring the limestone facades of the university buildings as they strolled by. The stone was stained and badly weathered on many of the buildings, but that only served to give them an extra layer of interest, or so Dykeman thought. What's more, whenever you touched any of the stonework, you were making contact with a long and glorious past, one that hundreds, maybe thousands, of other hands had likewise caressed over the course of many centuries. It gave him goosebumps thinking about it.

"Bloody old rubbish," grumbled Shapes as they passed the entrance to the Oxford Botanic Garden. "Should have pulled all these old buildings down years ago and put up something fit for modern living."

Dykeman ignored his grumpy sergeant, whose head still ached, and ambled on, happy as could be.

A swarm of students on push-bikes shot past them, sweeping down the gentle hill they were on and up over the bridge that crossed the River Cherwell a short way up ahead. Shapes grumbled something Dykeman couldn't make out, though what he was so bad-tempered about was impossible to say. What with the old stone buildings, the singing birds, the meandering river and everything else around them, this was, thought Dykeman, a little slice of paradise. Cole Porter was promptly added to the mix, as the Inspector ambled onwards.

Once over the river, they made their way up Iffley Road until they reached Temple Street, down which they turned. Most of the housing was of Victorian vintage, noted Dykeman. Small, well-kept, two-storey terraced places, where net curtains and polished door-steps proliferated. Number fifteen, their destination, was one of a pair of properties somewhat higher and wider than the others, which made it look a little ill at ease, to the observant eye of the Inspector.

While Shapes punched at the doorbell, Dykeman revisited his plans for the interview. Under other circumstances, he would have either phoned ahead to agree to an appointment or asked Oxford City Constabulary to pick up Wendy Slip and make a room available for the interview at the nearest station. But since she was, by all accounts, something of a lady of leisure, he was keen to make the most of the element of surprise. Never a bad thing to deny a suspect, or a witness, for that matter, the opportunity to prepare themselves for a few questions. Much too likely that, if they had something to hide, they would benefit from the advanced notice. Today, more than was normally the case, he wanted to see what reaction he got when he asked his questions.

The door opened and a man wearing a dressing gown and slippers looked out at them with an expectant look on his young face. He hadn't shaved, noticed Shapes, and his breath reeked of booze. Lucky bleeder, getting the chance to sleep in late after a heavy session on the town. He must, thought

Shapes, be a student. Who else lived such a life of care-free leisure in a university town?

"Can I help you?"

His voice was cracked, rasping, the words not fully formed.

"Inspector Dykeman and Sergeant Shapes," replied the senior policeman, holding up his warrant card. "We're looking for Wendy Slip."

The young man coughed and stretched his neck before risking a reply.

"Ah, Wendy has the upstairs flat. I'll show you up, if you like."

"She's in then, is she?" asked Dykeman.

"I believe so, yes."

"Good. On we go then."

The hallway and stairs were clean and, noticed Dykeman, looked recently decorated. The lack of dust and cobwebs suggested a cleaner was employed. How a student could afford such luxuries was anyone's guess. He couldn't afford one himself, not even on an Inspector's wage.

The unnamed man tapped on the single door on a small landing at the top of the stairs, then leaned forward so his face was almost touching the unpainted timber.

"Wendy, sweet. You have some visitors. Police officers."

The gentle sound of feet on carpet was soon followed by that of a turning lock and the door opened.

"I'll leave you to it," suggested the young man, who appeared to Shapes to be less than keen to do anything of the sort.

"Miss Wendy Slip?" asked Dykeman of the dark-haired beauty who stood before them.

"Yes, that's me."

"Inspector Dykeman and Sergeant Shapes. We'd like to ask you a few questions about Henry Graball."

Dykeman waved his warrant card under Wendy Slip's nose. She looked a little nervous, as if, thought Dykeman, she might have been expecting such a visit. It was, as was so often the case, the eyes that gave it away. Most people couldn't help themselves.

"You should come in."

Wendy Slip led the way along a short hallway into a sitting room, where they parked themselves on a two-seater sofa.

The flat, though small, was warm, tidy and didn't feel cramped, even with the three of them to accommodate. There was a faint whiff of perfume on the air; a floral number that Dykeman found rather appealing and distinctly feminine. He wondered if it was the sort of place Graball would appreciate or, perhaps, he had other things on his mind whenever he had chosen to pay a visit.

Dykeman studied Wendy Slip. She was sitting on the edge of an armchair, looking pensive, hands in her lap, shoulders a little hunched. On the way to Oxford, he had wondered how best to play this scene. One option was to not let on they knew she had been at Graball's party and then see if she would try to make out she hadn't been there. If she did, that would leave the obvious question; why? But she would need to be either stupid or desperate to try and pull the wool over their eyes like that, since her details had been recorded as part of the interview process following the murder and, surely, she would realise they knew that. In any case, he always much preferred to get right to the point.

"Do you know why we are here, Miss Slip?"

Tears welled in her eyes almost at once. Shapes sighed inside. Trying the old waterworks routine so soon. Well, she wasn't going to get away with sobbing. Him and Dykeman were too long in the tooth to fall for that old one.

"There, there, Miss Slip," came the soft words from Shapes's right. "Here, have my hankie. It's fresh."

Shapes turned his head, just a touch, to make sure he wasn't imagining things. He wasn't. What was Dykeman up to, the soppy sod? This had better be part of some cunning scheme to soften her up by acting so friendly.

"They wouldn't let me see him," she sobbed.

Shapes looked to the ceiling and shook his head. How many times had they seen this? A sharp pain in his ribs indicated a degree of unhappiness on the part of his boss. Shapes looked again to his right to find Dykeman frowning and shaking his head. Stupid old sod.

"He was quite a mess, I'm afraid to say. Best you didn't see him. And, of course, it was a crime scene, so we couldn't have anyone else in the room."

She dabbed at her eyes, leaving little smears of make-up on her lids.

"I'm told you weren't invited to the party. Is that true?" continued Dykeman.

"Yes," she said quietly, nodding her head.

"But you went along anyway? Why? Didn't you think that might risk a scene with Mrs Graball?"

"I... needed to go," she stumbled, fiddling with the hankie. "Such a big day for Henry. I just wanted to wish him well, in person. I couldn't stay away, not on such an important occasion."

"And did you get to see Henry Graball?"

"Yes," she nodded again. "I'd only reached the bottom of the stairs inside the main doorway. I wasn't sure which way to go, then he came down the stairs. It was as if he had sensed I was going to be there."

"And what was his reaction?"

Dykeman watched Slip's face closely, knowing they had reached the most significant part of the conversation so far.

"Well, to be quite honest, Inspector, he wasn't altogether pleased to see me. He worried his wife might see us together."

"A fair concern. So, did he ask you to leave?"

"Yes."

"But you didn't?"

"No. I couldn't, not so soon."

"Didn't he show you out?"

"No, he went into a room nearby to make a phone call, or to answer one. I can't remember which it was."

Dykeman's interest was piqued at once. The scene of the murder. Right location, right time. This was going to be interesting.

"What did he say when he saw you still there after he came back out of the room? He must have been annoyed. I hear he wasn't a man with a lot of patience."

"I wasn't there when he came out. Another man came along and got the impression I was lost. I didn't make any attempt to tell him I wasn't," she said, looking a bit sheepish, thought Shapes. "He took me through to the big room where the party was and I decided to stay there until Henry came back."

"Did you get the name of this man who took you through to the function room?"

"No, I'm afraid not."

"So, you didn't see Henry Graball again, after he spoke to you at the bottom of the stairs?"

"No."

"Did you see anyone else go into the room with Graball?"

"No, no one at all."

Dykeman paused, looking to one side to make sure that Shapes was keeping up with them as he scribbled away on his notepad. He also gave him a moment to consider his next question.

"Miss Slip, we have reason to believe Henry Graball had recently brought an end to his relationship with you. Is that true?"

"Oh, no. We had a little disagreement, that was all. We were far too close for Henry to do anything like that. He... well, he just got a little angry, nothing more. He was like that sometimes. Would say something he didn't really mean. But he always made up afterwards."

Dykeman noticed Wendy Slip seemed to be making an effort to perk up, seem more upbeat. Interesting thing to do. Perhaps he should persist with his line of questioning and see what might turn up.

"Our source was sure he was right. Heard it from the horse's mouth, so to speak. What do you say to that?"

Wendy Slip looked at her hands before answering. "Whoever this person is, I think they must have misunderstood the situation. Perhaps they weren't listening properly."

A strange way to put things, thought Dykeman. What with the lack of eye contact and the nervous movement of her hands, it seemed Wendy Slip was very likely telling a big fat lie. It seemed to him that the truth of things was all too obvious and the woman just couldn't face admitting it. Either that or she had some other reason for trying to convince them her relationship with Graball had remained intact.

"Is this flat rented?"

"Yes."

"Paid for by Graball?"

"Yes. He wanted somewhere nice for me to live. The place I was in when I met Henry was horrid. But that was Henry all over, he was so thoughtful."

"Where did the two of you first meet?"

"I used to work as a secretary at Union Street Steel Suppliers. Henry came in one day for a meeting with the managing director and noticed me, or so he said later. He phoned me the next day to ask if he could take me out for dinner that evening."

"Pretty brazen, asking you out like that when he'd not even spoken to you before."

"He was a very charming man, when he wanted to be, and every woman likes a little attention. He took me to the Running Brook in Cumnor. He was so sweet, I couldn't say no when he asked if we could meet again."

"What will you do now? I suppose you'll have to give up this place?"

"I don't know what I'll do. It's all so sudden. So..."

Tears began to fall again, more persistently than before. Wendy Slip dabbed the hankie at her eyes. Dykeman considered pushing on with further questions, but it looked unlikely they'd get sensible answers now; Wendy Slip looked too upset to string together more than a few words at a time. In any case, he felt they had already learned a good deal, not least that she appeared to be, as expected, infatuated with Henry Graball, despite his apparent short-comings. There was also this unnamed man who had come to her assistance. They would need to track him down and see if he could confirm her story.

"Can we get you a cup of tea, Miss Slip?"

"No, I'm fine, thank you," she replied, struggling to stem the tears.

"Well, in that case, we'd best not intrude on you any longer, Miss Slip. Thank you for your help."

They showed themselves out, leaving a sobbing Wendy Slip sitting alone in the flat. Dykeman couldn't fend off a little pang of guilt.

As they made their way along the pavement towards the Iffley Road, Dykeman asked Shapes for his assessment of what had just happened. "What do you reckon, then? Telling the truth?"

"No chance," answered Shapes, in a dismissive tone. "For one thing, that Underwood bloke was dead certain Graball had dumped her. And I mean permanent, like."

"I agree. She lied when I asked her about Graball ending their relationship, I'm sure of that. You could see it in her face and hear it in her voice. Perhaps she was hoping she could make him change his mind. I suspect she's still besotted with the man."

"If he had another woman already lined up, she would have had a hard time doing that. Anyway, I don't know what she's getting so upset about, you're not going to convince me that she was after anything more than as much of his money as she could get her hands on. What's more, with a pair of legs like she's got, she'll have no trouble finding herself a new fella to fleece."

"You're all heart, you are, Shapes. A regular romantic."

"Do my best, sir. Do my best."

As they turned the corner into Iffley Road, Dykeman decided it was probably a good thing his sergeant remained more than a tad cynical about Wendy Slip's motives, since he appreciated that he was himself probably guilty of being a little too soft on the woman. Perhaps between the two of them, they'd get it just right.

THE TRAIN RIDE BACK to Banbury was seized upon by Shapes as an excuse for a snooze, which might have been good for him, mused Dykeman, but the rest of the passengers in the same compartment were unlikely to have looked upon the situation in quite such a positive light given his sergeant's loud snoring. In the end, Dykeman woke his man from his slumber a stop early, having decided to take pity on those travellers who had not already moved to another compartment.

They were met by a car upon arrival and taken straight back to the police station, the Inspector keen to make the most of what remained of the day. He had a nasty feeling that those in a position of more authority than his would start to get restless if they didn't have some clear-cut progress to report soon. The Chief Inspector had already made his own views very clear, though Dykeman had considered that a straight-forward shot across the bows to make sure they got on with things. Another day, perhaps, and then things might start to get a bit uncomfortable for them if they hadn't got their teeth into something solid.

Dykeman was pleased to find the station a hive of activity, most of the work being carried out on his behalf. He'd initially intended both he and Shapes would catch up with the team that had been reviewing the horde of statements from the Conservative Club, but, as soon as they stepped on to the premises, the desk sergeant handed him a message to say Graball's accountant had called. Dykeman immediately instructed Shapes to call back the accountant, while he went to see if anything new had been gleaned from the statements. They would re-convene at his office to see where things stood. In the event, both men had something significant to report.

Chapter Six

Dykeman walked into the small office he shared with his sergeant to find Shapes sitting in his own chair, feet up on his desk, reading a copy of the Daily Express. A mug of tea sat on the edge of the desk, accompanied by a smattering of biscuit crumbs.

"Comfortable there, Shapes?"

"Certainly am, sir. Cup of tea there for you."

Shapes closed his newspaper and dropped it on the desk, before swinging his legs round in front of him as he turned towards Dykeman.

"Seems you're useful for something, after all. Anything interesting from that accountant, then?"

Dykeman shoved some papers out of the way and perched himself on his desk before sampling the tea Shapes had made for him. The smile that appeared on his sergeant's face was as welcome as it was unexpected.

"Indeed he did. Seems Henry Graball did a bit of banking on the side. Specialised in the business of loans. He especially liked punters who were strapped for cash. Ones he could charge high rates to."

"You do surprise me, Shapes."

"Always happy to oblige, sir."

"And there's one or two particular clients of Graball's we should be taking an interest in, I suppose?"

"Certainly is. He lent a load of money to an architect called Owen Plenty and it looks like things haven't worked out too well. The accountant says Graball was going to ask for his money back, knowing full well that Plenty can't pay up."

"I suppose there's a reason for doing that? What was Graball after, did the accountant say?"

"He did. Says it's the building the architect works from. Plenty owns it and would have had to hand it over to Graball if he couldn't come up with the readies."

"Well, well, well, looks like we have another suspect. Good job, Shapes. Where is this Owen Plenty's office?"

"Here, in Banbury, sir. South Bar Street."

"Good, we'll tootle on over there, after I've finished my cuppa. Now then, I've got some news too. Seems there was someone else who left the function room at the Conservative Club at the same time as Henry Graball. Someone we've already met."

Dykeman paused to give Shapes an opportunity to guess who the mystery individual might be.

"And who might that be, sir? We met a lot of people yesterday."

"It seems the Louches are a fidgety couple because it was Mrs Sheila Louch. Funny she didn't happen to mention that in her statement, or when we spoke to her."

"That's one way of putting it. Downright suspicious if you ask me. Makes you wonder if they might have finished off Graball together. They've got more reason than most."

"They do indeed, Shapes. Looks like we've got a busy afternoon ahead of us."

IT TOOK DYKEMAN AND Shapes a mere three minutes to drive the short distance from the police station to Owen Plenty's offices. The inspector might even have insisted they walk, if not for the fact they were planning to head off to the Louch residence afterwards. In any case, Shapes didn't like walking, something Dykeman was well aware of. The prospect of making him shed some shoe leather was a tempting one, but it would have to wait for another time.

Owen Plenty's practice operated out of a small two-storey premises on South Bar Street, a short distance from Banbury Cross. Built of limestone, with its warm, earthy glow, it was as typical an example of a seventeenth-century building as you'd find scattered across the town, mused Dykeman as they walked up the path towards the front door. Most of the neighbouring buildings were of a similar ilk and invariably occupied by either accountants, property agents or solicitors. It was a decent property, decided the inspector, and easy to see why it would be of interest to Henry Graball.

A young woman wearing a flower-patterned dress and a pair of thick black-rimmed glasses greeted them from behind a large wooden desk positioned to the left as they walked into the entrance hall. Her soft, rounded vowels identified her as a local lass to the ears of Shapes, who was instantly alarmed at the sizeable front teeth she exposed when she spoke. It made her look like she should be feasting on nothing but carrots.

Once Dykeman let the woman know who they were, the woman scuttled off to find her employer. Apparently he wasn't in the best of moods. Hadn't been for several days, all week even. No, she didn't know why, though assumed it was the pressure of getting their latest commission completed on time. They were behind schedule, despite Mr Plenty working extra hours.

"Inspector Dykeman."

Owen Plenty's educated tones announced his appearance to the two other men, both of whom were busy studying the entrance hall, out of habit as much as anything else. Both turned towards the tall, slender figure in the doorway at the rear of the hall. Shapes was immediately unimpressed by the modern two-piece brown suit and open-necked white shirt combo the man was wearing. He wouldn't be seen dead in such an outfit himself.

"Mr Owen Plenty?" asked Dykeman.

"That's me, Inspector. What can I do for you?"

"Is there somewhere private we can talk, Mr Plenty?"

"Of course. Do come this way. Er, can Erica get you a drink? Tea? Coffee?"

The two policemen declined the offer. They'd had their fill of tea for the time-being.

Plenty took them down a short, wide hallway to a room at the back of the building. In one of the other rooms they passed, Dykeman saw three men standing in front of vast draughting boards, each one apparently engrossed in the task at hand.

Plenty's office was bright, light flooding in through the two large sash windows that overlooked a large garden, most of which was laid to lawn. The room was, noted Dykeman, also extremely neat and tidy. Spartan, you might even say. Sign of a tidy, well-organised mind, the kind that could plan and execute a murder? Perhaps.

Plenty pulled two chairs into position in front of his desk, then sat down behind it in, what was to Shapes, an odd-looking chair. The top half swivelled, while the bottom half didn't budge an inch. To the sergeant, it didn't look right.

"What is it I can do for you, Inspector?"

Plenty had a full crop of dark blonde hair, which he parted from left to right, and possessed a pair of deep blue eyes. It was a combination which, added to his height and all-round good looks, Dykeman imagined made him popular with the ladies. Relevant to the investigation? It was hard to say, at this point.

"We understand you attended the party at the Conservative Club yesterday, for Henry Graball?"

"That's right, I did. I've known, or should say, I knew Henry for several years. Quite the turn out for him yesterday, though I still can't fully take in what happened. You don't think about such things happening in a quiet little town like Banbury."

If the man was feeling at all uncomfortable, thought Dykeman, then he certainly wasn't showing it. Instead, he looked and sounded entirely at ease. Still, they'd only just begun. Plenty of questions to be asked and answers to be given.

"You say years. Just how many years is that?"

"I first met Henry when I moved back to Banbury from London almost five years ago. I spent seven years working for a couple of big firms, learning my trade, you might say. But it was always my intention to set up a practice of my own. Wanted to pick and choose my own schemes and not have someone else telling me how to do my job. Henry was interested to hear about my ideas as to what constitutes good modern design practice and about a year later he gave me a commission for a new office building on the site of one of his premises in Oxford. It was a tremendous boost, you know. Raised my profile wonderfully well and brought in several other commissions in no time at all."

Dykeman wondered just what it was that lay behind Graball's decision to give a commission to such an inexperienced architect. From what they already knew of the man, he wasn't the sort to hand out work like Father Christmas. More likely, he had an ulterior motive from the start; one they were probably unlikely to discover now Graball was no more.

"And we understand that Mr Graball took a more direct interest in your business about twelve months ago, when he loaned you some money."

"He did, that's right. Although I had some funds of my own to invest, it wasn't really enough to grow the business as quickly as I wanted to. There's so much opportunity in this part of the country and, eventually, I intend to branch out across the whole country. I'd spoken to Henry about this several times and then, out of the blue really, he offered me a loan. Commercial terms, you understand, but rather more generous than I could get from any bank. The timing was exceptionally good, so I accepted."

"But things haven't gone so well since then, have they?"

"Well, there are always little bumps along the way when you are growing any business, Inspector. It's only to be expected."

At last, noted Dykeman, there was a hint of uncertainty in Plenty's voice. The man had tried to cover it up, but had not been completely successful.

"Little bumps, Mr Plenty? Just what sort of little bumps are we talking about?"

"I'm happy to help, inspector, of course, but I can't see how this relates to Henry's murder. Am I missing something?"

Dykeman smiled inside. Ah, the classic defence of someone with something to hide. Excellent.

"You must admit, Mr Plenty, someone who owes money, a lot of money, to Henry Graball is someone we should be speaking to, if only to cross them off our list of suspects."

Owen Plenty rubbed the fingers of one hand over his chin and glanced at Shapes, busy scribbling in his notepad.

"There were two commissions I had expected to win. I know we submitted the best bids, because the competition wasn't up to scratch. But, for some reason, we didn't win either. It left a rather large hole in our finances. I had to let one of the team go, but that wasn't really enough to fully plug the gap. It's not that we're idle, Inspector, just that our cash flow hasn't been what I expected it to be. That sort of thing is common in a growing business."

To Dykeman's mind, Plenty seemed overly keen to talk down his firm's troubles. It was noticeable how he'd started talking faster than before, as if he wanted to move things along as quickly as possible. Shame for him that, because the topic of conversation wasn't about to be changed any time soon.

"And I'm guessing Henry Graball wasn't exactly supportive when he saw you running into trouble."

Plenty fidgeted in his chair. He looked uncomfortable, thought Shapes, who was keen as mustard to hear how Plenty would answer that one. Make him squirm, sir.

"He could have been more understanding," replied Plenty, looking down at his desk. "He could see we've got a lot of business on our books. It's not as if we're twiddling our thumbs."

"He wanted his money back, didn't he, Mr Plenty?"

A little blush of red began to appear on Plenty's flawless cheeks, leaving Dykeman all the more confident he was on the right track.

"Well?" Dykeman pushed.

"Yes, he did. Told me I had a month to pay him back, or else."

Plenty's initial self-confidence was ebbing away fast, much to Shapes's delight. Could they be looking at the guilty man? Was he about to crumble under questioning?

"Or else what, Mr Plenty? What was Graball going to do if he didn't get his money back?"

Just like Shapes, Dykeman felt they were on the point of making a meaningful break-through. It was abundantly clear that Plenty was another individual with good reason to wish the businessman ill, but could this have developed into something far more deadly? Could Plenty have turned to murder?

"Mr Plenty?"

Owen Plenty let out a sigh and shook his head.

"He was going to take this building."

"He could do that, legally, I mean?"

"Yes, I had to put it forward as a guarantee against the loan. Graball would get ownership if I couldn't pay the loan back on time. It was due to be paid back last month."

The truth of things now out in the open, Dykeman decided he would give Plenty a moment to let the implications sink in and to consider his position. The inspector got to his feet, walked to the back of the room then turned around and walked back, resting his hands on the frame of the chair he had just vacated. He looked at Plenty with what he hoped was an unforgiving stare, before pressing on with the questions.

"At the party yesterday, you left the function room just before Mr Graball gave his little speech. Care to tell us where you went?"

"Nowhere particular. Just needed to get out of that room. I couldn't stand the thought of listening to Graball telling us all how brilliant he is. Made my stomach turn."

Interesting, thought Dykeman, there was some real feeling in that reply. It seemed the facade Plenty had originally presented to them had now all but collapsed.

"So, you weren't expecting amusing anecdotes and funny jokes about the mother-in-law. Seems no one else was either. All the same, you went somewhere. I don't imagine you just vanished in a puff of smoke."

"Didn't know where I was going. I just wanted to get out of that room. I don't really remember why I did, but I took the stairs to the top floor. There were some chairs there, so I sat down and had a smoke. All I've been able to think about since Henry demanded his money back is what that means for this business. I tried to push that to the back of my mind, focus on something more calming for a change, but I failed. I just sat there worrying."

"And you didn't go anywhere else until you went back down to the function room?"

Plenty didn't answer at first. He inspected the fingers on his right hand, wondering whether or not he should say anything more. He felt tense, aware sweat was accumulating in his armpits and there was an unpleasant taste in his mouth. The policemen seemed to think he had a good reason to commit murder and, under different circumstances, he would have agreed with them. The last thing he wanted to do now was fuel their suspicions. Maybe he should give them something to write down in that bloody notepad without implicating himself. Maybe then they would leave him alone.

"I heard voices coming from below. It was Henry and a woman, dark hair, pretty, as far as I could tell. They were arguing, though I couldn't make out enough of what they were saying to know what about. It looked pretty animated. Don't suppose there's anything new in Graball falling out with someone. A lot of us have been down that road."

"You couldn't make out any of what they said?"

"No, not really. Just the occasional word. I think Graball was telling her to leave. But I'm not sure."

Then it occurred to Plenty that he was in danger of missing a trick. It was obvious what he should say next. Why miss such a gold-plated opportunity to steer the police somewhere else, so they would leave him alone.

"She sounded pretty upset, though. Did make me wonder what kind of relationship they had. I'm sure a man like Henry wouldn't think it wrong to have a little entertainment on the side."

Dykeman and Shapes exchanged a glance.

"What happened next?" prompted Dykeman.

"Don't know, I'm afraid. I was thinking of going down there, to have it out with Graball, once the woman had left, but I knew it would be pointless. He's not the kind of man who changes his mind. So I stubbed out my cigarette and went back to the function room."

Dykeman pondered for a moment. It was almost certainly Wendy Slip that Plenty had seen arguing with Graball. That was helpful to know. It was a shame he hadn't seen how things ended. Had Graball gone into that room alone, or had Slip gone with him? Or perhaps he had seen her leave, after all, then made his way down the stairs and into the room where Graball was. The man had a motive, no doubt about that, and it looked now like he had the opportunity. But did he have the nerve? Was he the kind of man who would act on an impulse? Or was he someone who would need to plan out how he was going to kill? Architects didn't come across as impulsive. And why was he now looking so much more relaxed than he was a minute or two ago? Dykeman wondered if there was something he'd missed. Good God, their job could be frustrating at times. Before he could make up his mind what question to ask next, there was a timid knock on the door.

"See who that is, Shapes," commanded Dykeman.

The sergeant did as he was bid and opened the door. The young woman from reception stood there, wearing an apologetic look and holding her hands together in front of her chest.

"I do apologise, Mr Plenty, but Mr Crouch is on the phone and he really is most insistent he speaks to you at once, otherwise he says he's going to take his business elsewhere."

Plenty looked at Dykeman, but the inspector spoke before the architect could speak.

"It's alright, Mr Plenty. We've got enough for now. We'll let you know if we need to speak to you again."

"Thank you, Inspector. Erica, dear, tell Mr Crouch I'll be right there, please."

As the two policemen walked along the pathway towards their car, Plenty stood in the open doorway watching them go. He was a concerned man. The officers visit had not been a pleasant experience. Whilst they hadn't actually come right out with it and accused him of murdering Henry Graball, they might just as well have done. It was obvious from the line of questioning what they really thought. He rubbed his right temple and closed his eyes; he had another headache coming on.

Chapter Seven

Matthew and Sheila Louch lived in a semi-detached house on the southern edge of Banbury, on the road to Adderbury. Or, at least, they had done since Matthew Louch had found making a living rather difficult after Henry Graball's intervention in his affairs. To Dykeman's mind, eyeing up the front of the property as Shapes steered their car on to the drive, it was the kind of house most ordinary people would be only too happy to move into, though he had a strong suspicion the current residents didn't view things in quite such a positive light. Ungrateful idiots.

Shapes parked their vehicle slap bang outside the front door. No point, he decided, in giving the two of them an unnecessarily long walk. He might do himself an injury. It had happened before. Best not to take any chances. He climbed out of the car, looked up at the house and sniffed. Not so bad for people who were supposed to have fallen on hard times.

Dykeman looked across the roof of the car at his sergeant. The look on the man's face was a familiar one.

"Best behaviour, Shapes. And flush the toilet afterwards if you get an urgent need to empty your bladder."

Shapes turned to face his boss, one eyebrow raised in a look of astonishment. "Wouldn't dream of doing anything else, sir. Brought up proper, I was."

The front door was opened by Matthew Louch and it was clear from the strong smell of alcohol on his breath that he had been drinking. That he'd been drinking was even more obvious to the two policemen as they observed the erratic way Louch wandered along the hallway in front of them. Shapes wondered if there might be any chance of them getting a small one themselves. Never did any harm to ask.

The Louches had guests. Nigel and Anne Nettle occupied a small, floral-patterned settee on one side of the living room. They were discussing some aspect of gardening with Sheila Louch, who was sitting on the edge of an armchair opposite them. It was a conversation that ceased almost as soon as the two policemen entered the room.

"Inspector," declared Anne Nettle. "What a wonderful surprise."

The look of unbridled happiness that appeared on the faces of the Mr and Mrs Nettle immediately set alarm bells ringing for Dykeman. He would have to put the kibosh on their expectations forthwith. Bloody nosy parkers were something he could do without.

"Mrs Nettle. Mayor." said Dykeman in response, adding a civil nod of the head.

"How's the investigation going, Inspector? Any hot suspects?" asked Nigel Nettle, who was on his feet, offering his hand to Dykeman. The Inspector shook it with reluctance.

"It would be inappropriate of me to go sharing information like that, Mr Mayor. Things are moving along in a methodical manner, is all I will say."

"Nigel and I are both of the opinion it must have been some awful character who managed to break into the club. Aren't we, Nigel?" Anne Nettle didn't give her husband chance to answer. "Henry must have stumbled upon him trying to break into a safe or something of the sort and..."

"Well, I'm sure that's a possibility we'll be looking into, Mrs Nettle." Dykeman put an end to the chit-chat with what he felt was an admirable display of efficiency. "Now then, we're here to speak to Mrs Louch and we'll need to do that in private. If you don't mind..."

Dykeman gestured in the direction of the open doorway.

"Of course, Inspector. Understand entirely," replied Nigel Nettle, the disappointment clear in his voice, though not half so clear, noted Dykeman, as the look on his wife's face.

"Thank you for the tea, Sheila, dear. And do let me know if those dahlias are as red as they say they are."

Anne Nettle lingered for a brief moment, then followed her husband out into the hallway. Shapes followed and closed the front door behind them with a solid thump.

"I'm sorry about that, Inspector. Anne can be rather excitable."

Sheila Louch looked tired, thought Dykeman. Her eyes were darker than before and her voice quieter.

"That's no problem, Mrs Louch. We're used to that sort of thing, aren't we, Shapes?"

"Certainly are, sir."

Dykeman took a seat opposite Sheila Louch, while Shapes opted to remain standing to one side of the room. Matthew Louch, perhaps aware he wasn't any too steady on his feet, dropped on to the settee.

"Been friends of yours for long, have they?" asked the Inspector.

"Quite a while, yes. They've really been very good towards me and Matthew. Didn't treat us like lepers when the rumours started, unlike most of our other so-called friends. Anne can be a little tiresome at times, but she means well."

"Sounds just like Shapes."

Dykeman grinned at his sergeant, who chose not to rise to the bait.

"Can I get you and your sergeant a drink, Inspector. Tea? Coffee?"

Sheila Louch went to stand up but stopped, as Dykeman raised a hand.

"No, we're quite alright, thank you, Mrs Louch. We won't be keeping you long."

"Bloody chatterbox, that woman," slurred Matthew Louch, as if he'd only just caught up with the conversation.

His wife looked at him, her brow furrowed for a brief moment.

"We've been going through the interview notes from the guests at Graball's party and there's something we need to ask you about, Mrs Louch. In your own statement, you don't say anything about leaving the function room during the time

Henry Graball was absent, but in the statements of several other people they say they saw you leave the room shortly after your husband did."

Sheila Louch gave the matter some thought before replying. "I do apologise, Inspector. I thought I had told the constable. Yes, I did leave the room. After Matthew didn't come back for several minutes, I wondered what on earth he might be doing, so went to look for him."

Dykeman noticed a certain hesitation in Sheila Louch's speech, as though she might be holding something back.

"Worried he might have got lost?"

Sheila Louch looked down at her hands before answering.

"The truth is, Inspector, I was worried. Matthew really didn't want to be there. Not after what Henry Graball did to him. I thought Matthew might have left altogether. Started to walk home. I know it's difficult for him, but it's important, you see, that we do our very best to get back on our feet and not find ourselves complete outcasts."

Sheila Louch looked at her husband with a tenderness that Dykeman couldn't fail to notice. The woman clearly hadn't given up on her old man, even if it seemed he'd chosen to bury his head in a bottle.

"Did you find him?"

"No, I didn't. Some horrible-looking member of staff came storming round a corner in the corridor without looking properly where he was going. I'd taken my drink with me and he knocked it out of my hand. Most of it landed on my dress, so I had to make my way to the ladies toilets instead and clean myself up. By the time I'd done that, people were running around in panic. I suppose that's when Henry's body must have been found by then."

"And you went straight back to the function room after that?"

"Yes. Things were already rather confused, so I thought that would be the best thing to do. If Matthew hadn't left the building after all, then he was likely to make his own way back there sooner or later."

"You say you saw a member of staff in the corridor. Did you see anyone else?"

Sheila Louch thought for a moment, then shook her head.

"No, no one else. I could hear voices, but they were some way off."

Dykeman climbed to his feet and wandered over to a large, ornate sideboard. A collection of half-a-dozen photographs were grouped at one end. He picked one up and looked at it.

"Family photo?"

"Yes, that's our son, Anthony, and daughter, Joan. That's from a holiday in Scotland. They were both in their teens then."

"Do they still live here in the house?"

"No, they're both grown up now. Anthony lives in London and Joan moved to Oxford the year before last. We're hoping Anthony and his wife will provide us with our first grandchild soon, though we try not to pester them about it."

"Sheila's desperate to have little Louches running about the place," added Matthew Louch, smiling broadly. "Hundreds of 'em, if she can."

Dykeman put the photo back on the sideboard.

"Must have been very difficult for the two of you, dealing with the fall-out from Henry Graball's intervention in your affairs."

Sheila Louch produced a thin smile. Dykeman got the clear impression it took some effort not to snap back at him.

"We've battled our way through some very difficult moments, Inspector. I'm sure you can understand," came her careful and controlled reply.

"Sod 'em all," chimed in Matthew Louch, a look of disappointment on his face as he peered into his empty glass. "We don't need 'em. Stand on our own two feet."

His wife remained impressively calm, thought Dykeman. There were plenty of wives who'd be none too pleased at seeing their husbands in such a state when they had company. She seemed to read his mind.

"You'll have to excuse my husband. It's the stress. I'm afraid Matthew has found things very hard to deal with and sometimes goes looking for relief in a whisky bottle. Just so long as it doesn't become a regular thing."

She stared at her husband. Dykeman looked into her eyes, searching for clues as to what she might really be thinking, but all he found there was a steely determination.

"Were you surprised to get an invitation to the party from Henry Graball?"

"We were," replied Sheila Louch. "But I suppose we shouldn't have been. Graball was the kind of man who liked to rub your nose in it if he thought he'd got the better of you."

"But you accepted, all the same?"

"Yes. Matthew didn't want to. Said we should stay well away. It wasn't that I didn't feel as angry as he did, but I felt

Matthew needed to make the most of the opportunity to mix with the people who would be there. If he's ever to get back on his feet, he needs to keep himself in the minds of potential clients."

"I can understand that," responded Dykeman, glancing in the direction of Matthew Louch, who remained silent.

"It's not easy, Inspector, but we're determined not to be forced to move away. We brought our children up in this town and it's been our home since we married."

It would have been helpful to ask a few questions of Matthew Louch, thought Dykeman, but the man was clearly in no condition to provide proper answers. Amusing ones, perhaps, but nothing they could rely on. That was a shame.

"Did Henry Graball speak to you during the party?"

"No and I'm sure Matthew and I are both glad of that."

Matthew Louch mumbled something, but Dykeman couldn't make it out. It was, he decided, time to move on. He'd got the information he'd come for and more besides, whilst they still needed to return to the station.

"Well, we'd best be getting along, eh Shapes?"

"Sir."

"I'll show you out, Inspector. And I'm sorry again about forgetting to tell your constable I left the function room. I hope it's not caused you any problems."

"No need to fret, Mrs Louch. It's just tidying up one loose end, because we don't like those. They get in the way."

As she closed the front door behind the two departing policemen, Sheila Louch felt a sense of relief wash over her. She couldn't tell from the look on their faces what they might have been thinking during the course of their brief visit, but she was most definitely glad it was over. After all that her and Matthew had been through since he'd been forced to resign as mayor by Henry Graball, the last thing she wanted now was for the police to come around sticking their noses in where they weren't wanted. She and Matthew wouldn't survive another scandal.

Outside on the driveway, Dykeman and Shapes lingered either side of the car as the senior policeman asked his sergeant what he thought of their visit. Shapes hadn't yet had a chance to reply when the high-pitched sounds of an argument came from inside the house.

"Seems she's not as forgiving as I reckoned," smiled Dykeman.

"Hope he remembers to shove a phone book down the back of his trousers before she dishes out his punishment," replied Shapes. "I bet she don't take no prisoners."

"Jealous, Shapes?"

"Not this time, Sir."

BANBURY POLICE STATION was bathed in warm early evening sunlight as Shapes turned into the rear entrance to the car park. Inside, it wasn't half so bright and welcoming, thought Dykeman, but at least it was quiet. He wanted to compare notes with Shapes before the day was done. See what his sergeant reckoned to the conversations they'd had with Plenty and the Louches.

The small office they shared was, by comparison with the outside world, a dark, dank cave. Shapes flicked on the light switch and they both squinted in the resulting glare.

"Hello," announced Dykeman, as he stepped across the room to his desk. "We've had some calls."

He picked up two pieces of paper the duty sergeant had sent round from the front desk. One was a piece of news he'd been expecting, the other was not.

"Why don't people call us when we're in, instead of waiting until we've gone out?" asked Shapes.

Dykeman looked at Shapes but chose to ignore his sergeant's deeply philosophical observation.

"The Graballs's solicitor called. Mrs Graball gets all her husband's loot. He's left sweet Fanny Adams to charity or anyone else, come to that."

"Surprised?"

"Would be less surprised if the Pope announced she's a woman."

"What d'you reckon she'll do with all those shares in her husband's companies? Can't see her taking on things."

Shapes pulled a hankie out of a pocket and blew his nose. The sound echoed in the small room, causing glass panels to vibrate. Dykeman had already put his hands over his ears.

"Maybe one of their children will."

"If I was her, I'd flog the lot and move to the Caribbean. Get myself a bleeding great boat to go with my whacking great big house and move in a couple of the local girls. You'd never see me back here again."

"You trying to say you can live without me, Shapes? I'm hurt."

"Sorry, sir. I was forgetting about you. You could have a shed at the bottom of the garden. Suppose I could pay you a few quid to be my handyman."

"All heart, you are Shapes. Now then, this other message is a whole different kettle of fish. Seems Daphne Graball has found out about Wendy Slip."

"There'll be trouble now."

"Already has been. That student who let us in when we went to see Wendy Slip phoned in a report to say Daphne Graball's been round on the war path. Right old shouting match, by all accounts. Called each other some choice names and Miss Slip was told to clear off out of that flat tout suite. Very risky move by that student. Apparently he stepped in before they came to blows. No one hurt, just a few tears from Wendy Slip."

"Wonder who spilled the beans?"

"Some well-meaning friend, no doubt."

The look on Dykeman's face made it clear to Shapes that his boss thought otherwise.

"Bloody troublemaker, you mean."

"Indeed I do, Shapes."

Dykeman dropped the two slips of paper on to his desk, then sat down.

"So, what have we got then? Who had a reason to do in Graball?"

"Half the county, by the sound of things," replied Shapes, sitting on the edge of his own desk.

"Let's stick to those we know were at the club."

"Well, there was Matthew Louch. Graball pulled the rug out from under him. Plenty of reason there."

"That's true, revenge is a solid motive for killing someone. And the same thing is true for Owen Plenty."

"I don't like him. Seems fishy to me."

"I don't reckon he was telling us everything when we spoke to him. Got the definite feeling he was holding something back. If he thought Graball was a proper friend, trying to help him out with that loan, then he'd have plenty of reason to be feeling angry about the way he's been treated."

"I'd blow a gasket. Dig Graball's eyes out with a blunt stick."

Dykeman took his shoes off and wiggled his toes.

"I don't doubt for a moment, Shapes, that if you were a suspect I'd have you under lock and key by now. But could Plenty go through with something like that, even if he was desperate."

"We've locked up old ladies for doing in someone else, so I can't see no reason why Plenty couldn't be guilty of murdering Graball. He could be sitting in his office right now, smoking a cigar and congratulating himself on having seen us off."

"And then we've got Wendy Slip."

"Decent looker, she is. Old Graball did alright there."

"But don't forget he'd dumped her, or so we're told."

"Not according to her. Mind you, she sounded a bit desperate on that front, even if she did hope she could persuade him to take her back."

"Yes and that's what's nagging at me about that young woman. I don't think she's half as weak and feeble as she likes people to believe."

"Would like to have seen her and Daphne Graball going at it."

"Get your mind back on the case, Shapes."

"It is, sir. I meant, it would have been interesting to see who came out on top and who backed down."

"That's three people, all with a motive and every one of 'em left that function room shortly before Henry Graball was murdered."

"And don't forget about that waiter guy. The one Matthew Louch reckoned he saw arguing with Graball."

"You're right about that, Shapes. We should find out who he was and what they were arguing about. And we can't rule out Sheila Louch, either. She put on a convincing show when we spoke to her, but does anyone really forget to mention they left that function room when Graball was killed?"

"That's not bad, four or five suspects out of over a hundred and fifty people who were there."

"Four or five so far, Shapes. If what we've found out about Henry Graball is even half true, most of the people at that party could have had a good reason to stick the knife in."

"Suppose so."

Dykeman looked at his sergeant. The man had been unusually glum of late. Definitely not his usual self. What had happened to the grumpy Shapes he was used to working with every day? He'd not even noticed him ogling the young woman at Owen Plenty's office. Something was not right.

"You've been quiet the last couple of days, Shapes. Feeling a bit under the weather?"

Shapes's face didn't move a muscle. Long seconds passed before he spoke and, observed Dykeman, he seemed reluctant even then.

"It's my sister, sir. Says there's something dodgy going on at the massage parlour."

Ah, thought Dykeman, this could be amusing. Probably why Shapes hadn't said anything to him sooner.

"You mean that brothel she runs for the pair of you? What's up, some of the staff come down with a nasty dose of something unpleasant? Put the paying punters off, has it?"

"It's not a brothel, sir. Like I've said a hundred times before, it's a massage parlour."

Shapes sounded annoyed, much to Dykeman's amusement. If there was an honest-to-goodness massage parlour anywhere in the country then he had yet to hear about it. Shapes and his sister had inherited the business from an older cousin, one who had fled to Canada in a hurry after falling foul of the husband of a woman he'd been entertaining for several months. Seeing how the place was in the East End of London, Shapes and his sister had agreed she would run it, on account of her living in the city. Shapes had originally expected to retire on the proceeds within the year, but right from the start it never seemed to make more than enough to keep him housed and fed. Mind you, that wasn't something to be sneezed at.

"If you say so, Shapes. And what's the problem that's got you so bothered?"

"Someone's been causing trouble. Breaking windows, harassing the girls. My sister says she was followed home last night by some bloke in a long coat and hat. She was too scared to have a go at chasing him off, what with everything that's been going on."

"Your sister, scared? Things must be bad. From what you've told me about her, I would have thought lions and tigers would give her a wide berth. Hasn't she reported it?"

"Yes, she reported it after the front window got smashed in and the local bobby did a couple of walk-bys on his rounds for the rest of the week. But when it looked like things had quietened down, he went back to his usual route."

"You want to take some time off and head down to London? It's alright by me."

"Not yet. Not while we're working on this murder case."

"Well, how about we wrap things up here, then you get straight on the next train south and tootle off down to London to help sort things out? Shouldn't take a bloodhound like you long to work out who's been misbehaving."

"Thank you, sir. I'll let my sister know."

Dykeman slipped his feet back into his shoes and glanced at his watch. They'd had a long day. Although there was still much to be done, he was happy with their progress. They had earned themselves a beer and a decent night's sleep, which they'd need if they were to be sharp as pins the next day.

"Come on then, Shapes, I reckon it's time we went for a pint. Come to think of it, I could do with two. It's been a long old day."

"Sound idea, sir. And I wouldn't mind a steak pie to go with my beer."

Chapter Eight

"What have you got there, Shapes?"

Dykeman eyed with considerable suspicion the food his sergeant had brought back to their office from the station canteen. Shapes clearly thought it was suitable for breakfast. Dykeman considered it was just possible it contravened some sort of food hygiene by-law.

"Bacon, gherkin and salad cream sandwich, sir. Thought I'd try something a bit different. Don't like to get too set in my ways."

"You're disgusting at times, Shapes. I suppose we won't be able to go far from the nearest toilet after you've put that away."

"You're forgetting, sir, I've got a stomach like a cast-iron bucket. Bit of gherkin won't do me any harm. Want a bite?"

Shapes dangled one half of the offending sandwich in front of him. Dykeman flinched and made a face like an unhappy bulldog.

"I'd rather eat my own kidneys."

The phone on Dykeman's desk kicked into life. The Inspector picked up the handset and turned to face the wall, so he wouldn't have to look at Shapes's disgusting breakfast while he spoke.

"Dykeman here."

He heard a familiar and welcome voice on the other end of the line.

"Good of you to call back, Mr Louch. Yes, we'd like you to toddle along to the Conservative Club this morning. I've arranged for all the male staff to be on site so you can take a look at them. Would be a big help if you could identify the waiter you saw arguing with Graball."

Matthew Louch confirmed his availability.

"Excellent. Shall we say ten o'clock? Thank you, Mr Louch."

Dykeman dropped the receiver back in place with a satisfied flourish of the hand.

"Got a bit of a sore head, has he?" mumbled Shapes, one side of his mouth stuffed with bacon, gherkin and bread.

"On the contrary, he sounded in rude good health. Maybe he's got a stomach to match your own, Shapes. Anyway, he's going to meet us at ten, which means we've got twenty-five minutes. Wouldn't have thought he should have any trouble identifying this waiter. Sounded to me the other day like he got a pretty decent look at him."

"Think there might be something in it?"

"Who knows? If nothing else, we can cross the waiter off our list of suspects. Nothing else come out of all those witness statements, I suppose?"

Shapes shook his head and swallowed another mouthful of sandwich.

"Nope. The men are going through them a second time, just in case they missed anything, but I doubt we'll get anything else out of those. Looks like no one we've not already spoken to saw or heard anything that might be helpful."

"That's a shame. You know there's one thing we haven't worked out yet. There was a lot of blood in that room. Whoever murdered Graball can't possibly have got away without getting splashed with blood themselves, most likely a fair old bit. But no one in the club that day seemed to have so much as a speck of blood on their clothes."

"Maybe they took a change of clothes with them?"

"Possible. But would they have had enough time to get changed? And what happened to the original clothes, the incriminating ones?"

"Doesn't take all that long to change clothes and maybe we just haven't found them yet. It's a big building. They could have stuffed them into some dark corner in the back of a storage room. If it was one of Graball's guests, they would have had time to plan it all."

Shapes popped the last bit of sandwich into his mouth, chewed, swallowed and let out a satisfied belch.

"Good was it?"

"Think I'll have the same again tomorrow."

"I'm very pleased for you, Shapes."

"Cup of tea, sir?"

"As you're offering, but make it snappy. We need to get over to the Conservative Club and make sure everything is shipshape and Bristol fashion before Matthew Louch shows up."

THE TEN MINUTE WALK across town gave Dykeman and Shapes ample time to consider their options. They settled on putting two quid on Tony's Uncle in the one thirty-five at

Warwick races. They'd made a few quid on the horse the previous year and it had lost none of its form since then. Shapes was charged with lodging their bet as soon as they were done at the Conservative Club.

The general manager was waiting for them in the club entrance hall. To Dykeman's mind, the man appeared far too keen on ushering them out of sight of any members who happened to be on the premises. As it was, they saw few other people between the entrance hall and the large ground-floor room at the back of the building that had been commandeered for their use.

PC Dartington met them outside the room.

"We all ready then, Dartington?" asked Dykeman.

"We are, sir. There's ten men who were working here on the day Mr Graball was killed. We've got them all here."

"And Matthew Louch?"

"He's in that room over there, waiting for us to call him."

"Good. Right, let's have a look at this lot before we get started."

The room was large, some twenty-feet long and half as wide. It looked to the inspector as though it might once have been some sort of office. A single, dust-covered desk loitered in a corner. The room seemed now to be used for storage of sundry items, such as boxes of new staff uniforms and various laundry materials.

A line of men stood along one side of the room, some looked unhappy, some disinterested and two, who were deep in conversation, were actually smiling. They had all denied being the man seen by Matthew Louch arguing with Henry Graball.

Dykeman ran an eye over all ten and was pleased to note the lack of similarity between them. There was a variety of heights, hair colours, body sizes and even nose shapes. The age range also offered plenty of scope for identification purposes.

Happy things were in good order, Dykeman gave a nod to Shapes, who then stepped into the middle of the room, facing the assembled throng.

"Right then, let's have your attention. I'm Sergeant Shapes and this is Inspector Dykeman. We won't be keeping you long and all you need to do is stand in a nice straight line while PC Dartington here brings in a gentleman who is going to cast an eye over you. I don't want any talking or mucking about. Just stand there nice and quiet."

There was a little shuffling as the line straightened up. No one else spoke, which Shapes was happy to put down to his authoritative direction.

"OK, Dartington, bring in Mr Louch."

Matthew Louch, noted Dykeman, seemed to have gone to some lengths to make sure he was dressed to impress; or perhaps Mrs Louch had insisted on it. He was wearing a very nice three-piece brown suit with matching tie. His brown shoes glistened so brightly they might have dazzled some folk.

"PC Dartington explained things to you, Mr Louch?"

"Yes, thank you, Inspector. Shall I begin?"

"Don't hold back on my account." replied Dykeman, waving Matthew Louch forward.

The new arrival stepped forward without hesitation so that he was directly in front of the first man in the line and took a careful look at his face. As he made his made his way down the line, Matthew Louch stopped right in front of each man, stared for a moment at his face, then cast an eye over the rest of him. An impressively thorough approach to things, noted Dykeman, happy their witness could not be accused of being slapdash. Once he'd finished appraising the last man in the line, Louch turned towards Dykeman, nodding gently.

"Is the man you saw arguing with Henry Graball here, Mr Louch?"

"He is, Inspector."

"Would you mind pointing him out?"

Matthew Louch stepped back along the line until he came to a short, balding man who, noted Dykeman, was fidgeting in a manner that suggested he was far from comfortable. Excellent.

"It was this man," said Louch, placing a hand on a shoulder.

"I ain't done nothing," squawked the nervous-looking man, brushing away Louch's hand. "You ain't blaming me for it. I don't care what he says, I ain't done..."

"Enough." snapped Dykeman. "Thank you, Mr Louch. If you wouldn't mind, please wait outside with PC Dartington, in case we need to speak to you again. The rest of you lot can get back to work. Thanks for your time."

The nine unwanted men shuffled their way out, every last one of them, noted Shapes, casting a suspicious eye at the colleague who had been made to stay behind. They were like schoolchildren who wondered what their misbehaving classmate had done wrong.

The door closed behind them and Dykeman wasted no time, turning to face the remaining man. Shapes was already poised with notebook and pencil, keen as mustard to hear what the fella had to say for himself.

"Right then, sir, what would your name be?"

"Sydney Tinkler, Mr Inspector." replied the man, his reluctance to provide an answer clear in his voice. He shuffled his feet and looked, for a moment, at the ground.

"And what's your job here?"

"Waiter, sir."

"And how long have you been waiting here?"

Dykeman couldn't resist the cheap joke. Shapes nodded his head in appreciation. Tinkler either didn't notice the attempt at humour, or else chose to ignore it.

"I've been working here ten months, sir."

Tinkler fingered his thinning, grey hair and watched Shapes as the sergeant scribbled on his notepad.

"You like it here, do you? A good employer, this place?"

"It's alright. Done worse jobs in me time."

"Same goes for Shapes, here. He's done a lot worse in his time. Just for the record, can you confirm you were one of the staff on duty during Henry Graball's party?"

"I was, sir."

"Not a nice man, we hear."

Dykeman made sure he was watching Tinkler closely as he asked the question, keen not to miss any change in the man's facial expression. It was almost impossible even for the best liars to avoid giving away their true feelings before realising what they had done. A little lifting of an eyebrow or colouring of the cheeks could tell an observant policeman a good deal.

"Who's that, sir?"

Well, that one didn't get a bite, noted Dykeman, with some disappointment.

"Henry Graball. We hear he wasn't what you might call considerate and understanding. Tended to trample all over people, in fact."

"Don't know about that, sir."

"But we have a witness who says he saw you having a heated argument with Graball. Or do you deny that was you?"

Tinkler sniffed and started tapping a heel on the wooden floor. It seemed to Shapes the man didn't realise he was doing it.

"That's right, sir. Mr Graball wasn't happy with the drinks I took to his table. Gave me some verbals."

"And you didn't agree?"

"I didn't. They was the right ones. I know it for a fact. Told him so, too. One gin and tonic for the mayor's wife and a whisky for Mr Underwood."

"How did he respond to that?"

"Started shouting at me, he did. Weren't no good reason for it. Said he'd get me sacked too."

"All very upsetting, I'm sure."

"It was that. Put me right out, it did."

"You had any problems with Mr Graball before? Any other run-ins about drink or food orders? I understand he was a frequent visitor to the club."

"No, nothing, sir. I saw him around, 'course, but never spoke to him."

Dykeman took a couple of steps to one side, hands in pockets, as he weighed up where best to go next with his questioning. If there was more to the argument Tinkler was seen having with Henry Graball, the waiter wasn't giving anything away.

"Where did you go once Graball had finished with you?"

"Back to the function room, sir. Couldn't be staying away any longer. Too busy for that."

"And what about Mr Graball? Did you see where he went?"

"He went downstairs, I think. Well, I saw him downstairs a bit later."

"How much later?"

"Well, maybe five or six minutes. But I ain't sure. I was taking some dirty plates back to the kitchen and I saw him standing at the bottom of the stairs."

"Was anyone with him?"

"Not what I could see. But I wasn't looking, see. I had my work to do."

"Did you see him again after that?"

"No, next thing I knows, he's dead. Here, in the club."

Tinkler sounded genuinely shocked, as if the idea that someone could be murdered in the Banbury Conservative Club was the most outrageous thing in the world.

"I'll tell you what, though," added Tinkler, his whole demeanour changing in an instant. "I did see someone coming out of that room where Mr Graball was murdered."

Dykeman thought he'd misheard at first, such was his surprise at Tinkler's statement. Could they really have got that lucky? He tried not to give away his immediate sense of joy.

"You did? And who might that have been?"

Shapes stood poised, his pencil ready to write down the incriminating words.

"Oh, I don't their name. It was a woman. Young one. Black hair, down to 'ere." He put a hand on his right shoulder. "Nice clothes. Bit of a looker, I'd say."

Dykeman and Shapes exchanged a glance. It was clear to both men they were thinking of the same woman.

"And did you see Henry Graball come out of the room with her?"

"No, just the young lady."

"And how would you say she seemed?"

"Don't rightly see what you mean."

"For example, did she look upset, as if she might have been arguing with Graball?"

"Not that I noticed. She just walked off."

Dykeman wrinkled his nose and scratched behind an ear. He couldn't go putting words in the man's mouth, but he felt this was significant news and he wanted more from Tinkler. Something that might suggest Wendy Slip was guilty of more than simply arguing with Henry Graball. After all, up to now she was the only other person, apart from the dead man, anyone had seen go into or come out of the room where Graball's body was found.

"You sure you didn't see anyone else go near the room?"

"I'm sure. No one."

Ah well, thought Dykeman, at least they finally had got something to get their teeth into. It was time for them to make another trip to Oxford; only this time their conversation with Wendy Slip wouldn't be in the cosy confines of her own home.

"Thank you for your time, Mr Tinkler. You've been very helpful."

As soon as Shapes had closed the door behind a relieved-looking Tinkler, he turned to face his boss, eager to confirm their next steps.

"We going back down the road to Oxford, are we?"

"We certainly are, Shapes. Looks like Miss Slip wasn't being entirely honest with us and she's got some serious explaining to do. I'd say things aren't looking any too good for her right now. But I also want you to get someone to take a look into Tinkler's background. Seems odd to me he would have a slanging match with a member of the club about a round of drinks. I'd have thought that's the sort of thing that could get him sacked."

"Don't trust him then, sir?"

"Let's just say I'd like to make sure we don't leave any stones unturned."

Chapter Nine

The two Banbury policemen arrived back in Oxford shortly before noon and made their way to the Oxford City Police headquarters without delay, despite Shapes suggesting they get some lunch first. Dykeman knew an empty belly made for a grumpy sergeant, but he was too keen to speak to Wendy Slip to be willing to give in.

Before leaving Banbury, Dykeman had phoned the Oxford police, asking them to pick up Wendy Slip and show her the hospitality available at the station. Perhaps the intimidating confines of a police interview room would make her less forgetful than she'd been at her own home.

"Hello Dykeman. Got us doing your work for you now, have you?"

Detective Inspector Graham Whistler was a former colleague of Dykeman and Shapes at Banbury police station. A big, rotund man with a bulbous nose and short grey hair, he had a handshake that gripped like a vice. Even though Dykeman was ready for it, he still found his fingers crushed. It took a good deal of effort not to wince.

"Need to make sure you lot have something to keep you busy, Graham. How's tricks?"

"Got the Home Secretary visiting tomorrow. Right palaver. We'll have so many men babysitting him that every crook in the city will be able to help themselves to whatever they want. Bloody ridiculous."

"That's what you get for moving to the big city. I bet the Home Secretary doesn't even know where Banbury is."

"You've had some press coverage with Henry Graball's murder though. How are things going? Hoping this Slip woman can help you?"

"Well over a hundred people on the premises at the time, would you believe. And seems more than one or two had plenty of reason not to like Graball."

"From what I've heard, he had more enemies than friends. There's people here who aren't exactly unhappy to see him gone."

"Sounds about right. Hasn't made it easy going for us, but we got our first really decent lead this morning. Someone saw Wendy Slip leaving the room Graball was found dead in. Funny thing is, she didn't mention that when we spoke to her yesterday."

Whistler sucked in air through his teeth.

"That doesn't look good. Wonder what she'll have to say about that?"

"You picked her up?"

"We have. She's waiting for you. Looks nervous, so I'm guessing she knows you've found out she went into that room with Graball. Means she's had time to think about it, mind.

Could have dreamed up some sort of plausible excuse that avoids making her look guilty."

"That's no problem. I'll just leave her alone in the room with Shapes. She'll talk soon enough."

"He still taking the mickey out of you, Shapes?"

"Sign of affection, or so the Inspector says, sir."

"Well, remember, when you've had enough of it, there's always a job for you here. Come on then, I'll take the two of you through to the interview room. Coffee? Tea?"

"Tea for me, sir," came the immediate answer from Shapes. "Any chance of a few biscuits?"

Whistler laughed.

"I'll see what we can do, Shapes."

WENDY SLIP WAS SITTING behind a small wooden desk that had, observed Dykeman, seen better days. The room had no windows and was lit by a single, very bright lightbulb suspended from the ceiling. Slip looked uncomfortable, nervous, fiddling with her fingernails. That was a good sign, decided the Inspector, one that suggested she appreciated the tricky nature of her situation. And tricky, it certainly was.

The two policemen sat down opposite Slip, without saying a word, Dykeman taking a deep breath and straightening his back. He glanced at Shapes, who nodded once as he produced his notepad and pencil from a pocket of his jacket.

"Well, Miss Slip, we meet again. And so soon after our first meeting."

She tried to look Dykeman in the eye, but was unable to sustain the effort required, so she looked at Shapes instead, before deciding she'd rather stare at the top of the table.

"Hello, Inspector." She spoke quietly.

"Would you care to hazard a guess as to why you're here?"

She glanced up at Dykeman and shook her head.

"I don't know. They didn't tell me. Have you found out who murdered Henry?"

"That depends."

Dykeman left it at that for the moment, wondering if the silence might unnerve her enough to say something more, preferably something incriminating. Let her stew a bit. Slip opened her mouth, then closed it again. Dykeman chose to maintain his silence. He could feel the tension in Slip and felt sure she was on the point of crumbling. Unfortunately, the silence was broken by an ear-piercing explosion from his left. Shapes had sneezed. Dykeman's ears rang.

"Sorry, sir. Must be a bit of dust in the air."

Dykeman gave his sergeant a look of displeasure, then turned back to Wendy Slip, disappointed to see that some of the tension he'd detected appeared to have left her. Damn it, why couldn't Shapes have held back his sneeze for a little longer?

"Bless you, Sergeant," offered Slip.

"You see, Miss Slip," said the Inspector in an effort to keep them on track. "We've been busy, me and Shapes. Spoken to a lot of people since we last met. Made some interesting discoveries. For example, it turns out someone was seen leaving the room where Henry Graball's body was found. Don't suppose you'd know anything about that?"

Dykeman brought his hands up on to the table in front of him and gave Slip what he considered to be a hard, penetrating stare, hoping it might review her feelings of discomfort. A little patch of pink flushed in the centre of her cheeks. Excellent, thought Dykeman. They were indeed on the right track.

"I think I owe you an apology, Inspector." Slip's head bowed a little as she spoke..

"And why might that be?"

"I suppose someone saw me coming out of that room... the one Henry..."

"Go on, Miss Slip."

"Oh, Inspector, I'm so sorry. I... I was scared. I thought you'd never believe me if I said I'd been in that room with Henry and... he was still alive when I left. I promise you, he was still alive."

Slip spoke with passion and, thought Dykeman, a degree of what he could only describe as fear, but she'd barely got the words when she burst into tears, sobbing into her hands. Shapes produced from a jacket pocket what Dykeman hoped was a clean hankie and handed it to Slip. She dabbed at her eyes, but the tears kept flowing.

Dykeman gave her a moment to compose herself, then decided to push on anyway.

"And what are we supposed to think when you keep that information from us, Miss Slip? Not exactly the sort of thing an innocent person would do, wouldn't you agree?"

He watched as Shapes drew a little noose on his notepad.

In between the tears, Wendy Slip continued with her plea. "You must believe me, Inspector, I would never harm Henry. Never. Let alone..."

"Well, someone killed him, Miss Slip. Stabbed him to death in a frenzied attack. Just the kind of thing a jilted lover might do. Wouldn't you agree, Shapes?"

"Certainly is, sir. And Miss Slip is the only person we know for sure went in that room with Mr Graball."

Shapes wanted to sneeze again. He pinched his nose until it hurt. The sneeze retreated.

"No, no. I couldn't, Inspector. Not to Henry. Not ever. You must believe me. I couldn't do... that."

The tears flooded down her face now, leaving black stains on her cheeks where her eye make-up had run. Turning on the waterworks was a tactic men didn't normally get the benefit of, thought Dykeman. But he'd been on the receiving end of that sort of thing too often to be softened by it.

"Shapes reckons you lost control of yourself when Mr Graball refused to have you back. There must have been a knife handy in the room and before you realised what you'd done, Henry Graball had signed his last cheque. A crime of passion. It's happened to plenty before you."

She shook her head again, trying now to choke back the tears, with some success. Red-rimmed eyes looked across the table at him, almost begging him to believe. But was she begging because she was guilty or because she was desperate to prove her innocence, wondered Dykeman.

The problem was, mused the inspector, that whilst they could put her in that room with Graball, they couldn't actually prove she killed him. They hadn't yet found the murder weapon, so had no chance to lift finger-prints, and there'd not been anything on the day to point to her being guilty. If it was her and she had taken a change of clothes... but then it would mean she'd planned it in advance. But how would she have known she could get Graball all alone? She could have taken a chance on it, of course. If only they could find the damned murder weapon.

"Henry never meant to hurt me, I know he didn't. He would have taken me back. He... he loved me, Inspector. He loved me."

She trailed off, her head dropping forward so her chin pressed against her chest. Did she really still believe that, wondered Dykeman, or was it dawning on her that Graball pretty much didn't seem to care for anyone but himself? That seemed to be the view of most other people, but was she only now coming round to the same point of view?

"Do you really believe that, Miss Slip? You really think Henry Graball would have taken you back after he'd dumped so many other mistresses before you?"

Slip covered her face with hands and there was silence, apart from the sound of her sobbing.

"Why did you go into that room, Miss Slip?"

It took a moment for her to recover enough self-control to answer, pulling her face up out of her hands. She looked lost, no longer sure where she stood, a sadness in her eyes that hadn't been there before. Hard-nosed though he considered himself to be, Shapes felt a moment's pity. That couldn't be allowed. He swept it up and shoved it back into a deep, dark corner.

"We argued, on the stairs."

"So you said before."

"Henry told me to leave, but I couldn't. I just stood there for a while after he went into that room, the one where... I couldn't believe he really wanted to end things, so I followed him. But... he wasn't very nice to me. Said things he'd not said to me before. I think I saw him angry then for the first time, really angry, I mean. It scared me, so I left."

"And there was no one else there with Graball"

"No."

"Did you..."

Dykeman's next question was brought to an abrupt end by a loud knock on the door. It was opened before he could answer by a young constable, who at once stepped into the room.

"It's Banbury, sir. PC Dartington says it's urgent. He needs to speak to you right away."

DYKEMAN AND SHAPES were sitting either end of a desk in a long, narrow office where half a dozen other officers were busy working. The Inspector had just finished his conversation with Dartington.

"Well, Shapes, there's good news and there's bad news."

"Good news first please, sir."

"They've found the knife used to kill Graball. It had been dumped in the bottom of an umbrella stand in the cloakroom. That's across the hallway from the room where he was killed. They've also found the coat that was reported missing. That was also in the cloakroom, splattered with blood. I think we can assume for now it was Graball's blood."

"So that explains how the killer managed to avoid getting blood on any of their own clothes."

"Yes, but that's where the good news ends. Apparently there are no fingerprints on the knife." Dykeman wrinkled his nose. "Suppose that would have been asking too much. Still, we got the weapon. That's progress."

Shapes was feeling pretty upbeat, but he couldn't help noticing that Dykeman had started drumming his fingers on the desk. Something was bothering his boss.

"Don't you reckon it's her then, sir? Miss Slip, I mean."

Dykeman blew air between his lips and tapped his chin with an index finger.

"I don't know, Shapes."

"But she had a motive and the opportunity, she's said as much herself. She's hardly going to stick her hands up and say, 'It's a fair cop', is she now?"

"It's that first time we spoke to her that's nagging at me. I got the impression she really did believe she could persuade Graball to take her back. I don't mean she was hopeful, I mean she really believed it."

"Apart from the little matter of him being dead and all."

"Ah, you might be right, Shapes. Maybe I shouldn't be giving that so much credence."

"Going soft, you are. It's messing up your head."

Dykeman glanced at his watch.

"Come on, there's one more question I want to ask Wendy Slip before we're done here."

Chapter Ten

By the time Dykeman and Shapes arrived back in Banbury, they both wore satisfied smiles. These were, however, only in part due to the success of their second interview with Wendy Slip. The other reason for their happy condition was that they had finally managed to fill their empty stomachs with sandwiches purchased on the way. Shapes had reached such a state of hunger he was worried he might need medical attention. As it was, they felt fully prepared to re-commence their work. Which was fortunate because it was already well past two o'clock and Dykeman had decided they needed to make at least two more visits before their afternoon's work could be considered at an end.

They stepped out of the railway station to find the sun had slipped behind a bank of fluffy, white clouds, though it was still pleasingly warm. Constable Johnston was waiting for them with a police car, as arranged. They dropped him back at the police station, then set off across town for Owen Plenty's office.

As Shapes pulled out from behind a small lorry and roared past, he half-turned his head towards Dykeman, "Good job you asked Wendy Slip to describe the bloke who walked her back to the function room."

"I had an inkling who it was she would describe," replied Dykeman. "We've heard so many lies already, one more is hardly a surprise."

"Can't wait to see the look on Owen Plenty's face when we tell him we know he went down those stairs, just like he said he didn't."

Dykeman gripped the handle on the door a little more tightly and looked down at his feet as Shapes continued on at an alarming speed.

"Yes, I'm glad we went back in to ask her about that. Our architect friend has some serious explaining to do."

"Bet he reckons he's pulled the wool over our eyes. Smart types like him always think they're too clever for the rest of us."

Shapes pulled the car to a sharp halt outside Plenty's office, causing Dykeman to slap a hand on the dashboard so he could support himself and avoid plunging forward. He muttered an obscenity under his breath. Shapes heard but pretended not to. Dykeman always reckoned he drove too fast, even when he was poodling along, like he had done this time.

The young woman they had met on their previous visit greeted them again. She was reading a novel and munching on an apple. She put the book down as they closed the door behind them.

"Oh," she said, a look of surprise on her face. "It's Inspector Dykeman, isn't it?"

"That's right. Mr Plenty here?"

"No, I'm afraid not. He's out on site. It's a new house in Middleton Cheney. He's expected back later this afternoon, if you'd like me to give him a message."

She had a nice smile, thought Shapes, though her teeth were too big. Would be dangerous to risk a kiss with her, if he ever got the chance.

"Is there an address for this house?" asked Dykeman.

"Yes, I'm sure it's here somewhere."

The young woman got up and opened a filing cabinet next to the desk. She pulled a large buff-coloured folder from out of the top drawer and leafed through it with great care, as if afraid to damage any of the contents.

"There we are. It's on the Chacombe Road, a little way up from the petrol station, I believe. I shouldn't imagine you'll have any trouble spotting it. Quite the building site at present."

She slipped the folder back in the cabinet and closed it.

About to leave in search of Plenty, it then occurred to Dykeman they ought to make the most of the visit, especially with Plenty out of the office.

"How's he been lately, Mr Plenty? Understand he's under a fair bit of pressure."

"Poor man. He works so hard trying to expand the business, but things have been very difficult of late. Commissions have been so hard to come by. I think sometimes it gets him down, though you can hardly blame him, of course."

"Does he tell the rest of you much about how things are going?"

"Not the details. I don't suppose that's for us to know. But we can all see things are difficult."

"Did Henry Graball ever come here to see Mr Plenty?"

"Henry Graball? Oh, he's that man who was murdered at the Conservative Club," she said, a little edge of excitement in her voice. "Did Mr Plenty know him? He never said."

"They'd met several times, we're told."

"Oh, I didn't know that. No, I don't think Mr Graball ever came here, or, at least, not when I was working. I suppose he could have popped in some other time. Mr Plenty does sometimes work late, after the rest of us have gone home."

"Well, thank you for your time. I guess we'd best get going, otherwise we might find ourselves passing Mr Plenty on the road, eh, Shapes?"

"Sir."

"I'll let him know you called anyway, Inspector. Just in case you do miss him."

They left the young woman in a state of some excitement, observed Dykeman. He had a firm suspicion their second visit and mention of Graball would be the topic of much conversation that evening when she went home to her family. Perhaps he oughtn't to have said anything about Graball, but it was too good an opportunity to pass up, even if it did fail to add anything to their store of knowledge. Oh well, ever onwards.

A WIND WAS BLOWING across the ridge on which Middleton Cheney sits and it tugged and snapped at the two policemen's clothing as they walked towards the building site where they hoped to find Owen Plenty. The house was little more than half-built, the first joists of the roof being put into place that afternoon, and piles of bricks, stacks of timber and sundry other items made for a decent obstacle course.

Shapes liked building sites. There was something about them that had appealed to him since he was a young boy and he sometimes thought he ought to have been a bricklayer or a carpenter. The nearest he'd ever got was helping his dad re-point a section of brick wall in the outbuilding where they kept their chickens. His dad told him he'd done a fine job, the best there ever was, but when he'd gone to inspect it one time as an adult, he saw what a rubbish job he'd done, the pointing jagged and uneven. But that hadn't dimmed the appeal. Maybe when he retired he could practise until he got good at it, then spend his hours building brick walls for anyone who wanted one.

The site foreman had seen them coming. He stood by a small hut, a mug of something steaming in one hand.

"Good day gentlemen and what can I do for you?"

"Inspector Dykeman and Sergeant Shapes. We were told we can find Owen Plenty here."

"Mr Plenty you want, eh?" he replied, rubbing the back of his free hand across his mouth. "He's round the back with some of the men. Had a problem with one of the doorways. Here, I'll take you there. Need to be careful on a building site, you do. Dangerous places to those what don't know 'em."

Shapes and Dykeman found Owen Plenty in an agitated mood. He was standing with a tall, broad-shouldered man with scraggy brown hair and forearms like tree-trunks, who was getting the worst of it fired at him. Plenty looked up, saw them heading his way and dismissed the builders around him. The foreman didn't wait to be dismissed and was gone before Dykeman could offer his thanks.

"Bit of a problem, is it?" Dykeman asked Plenty.

"Damn doorway. They've put it in six inches too far to the right, which means now we can't get the proper clearance we need for one of the inside doors. The whole lot will have to be re-done and that will mean more expense. More to the point, it will cost me money, because I can't pass on the extra cost. Fixed price contract, you see."

He brushed dust off the sleeves of his jacket and forced a smile, as if to suggest it was all part and parcel of a normal day for him. Neither policeman was fooled by that.

"We need to ask you some more questions, Mr Plenty. Seems you weren't entirely been honest with us when we last spoke."

Dykeman fixed Plenty with what he liked to think was a piercing stare.

"Not quite sure I understand you, Inspector. In what way was I not honest?"

Dykeman noticed Plenty glance around, seemingly concerned to ensure there was no one nearby. There wasn't, though, thought the policeman, that didn't mean they couldn't be overheard.

"Mr Plenty, you told us you didn't go down the stairs at the Conservative Club after you witnessed Henry Graball arguing with a woman you didn't recognise, but we now know that you did. What I want to know, Mr Plenty, is why you lied to us about that."

Dykeman stood so close to Owen Plenty they were almost toe-to-toe. He hoped the architect found it intimidating.

Plenty's head dropped forward and he briefly closed his eyes, before looking back up at Dykeman. "I thought you'd assume the worse. Think I killed Henry."

To Dykeman's ear, Plenty sounded like a defeated man. The trouble was, that could all too easily be a show, put on for their benefit. Another attempt to put them off the scent by giving them a little something, while keeping back the real meat of the matter. Dykeman wasn't going to have that.

"Come off it, Mr Plenty," snapped the Inspector. "You had a damn good reason to murder Graball and, it turns out, you also had the opportunity. Lost your temper, did you? Tried to persuade Graball one more time not to call in his loan and then lost control when he refused?"

"No. No. I didn't..."

"Couldn't face the prospect of losing your business? Laugh at you, did he? Rub your nose in it?"

Dykeman was right in Plenty's face now, his breath washing over the architect in waves. The Inspector felt a little exhilarated, so close to a possible confession. Push, push, push, he told himself. Break down those defences. Get a confession.

"No, Inspector. No..."

"Did you take the knife with you?" pressed Dykeman. "Or did you find it there? Grabbed it on an impulse? Then stab, stab, stab, in it went. Must have felt good, a relief almost, to let out all that frustration and anger. Did he beg for his life, Mr Plenty? Did he give you the pleasure of begging?"

"No, Inspector. Please, I swear to you, I did not murder Henry Graball," insisted Plenty, rubbing his face with one dirty hand. "I..." Plenty hesitated.

"You what, Mr Plenty? You never meant to do it?"

Plenty looked into Dykeman's eyes. Was that sadness the Inspector saw there, or something else? What was it?

"I wanted to face up to him again, that's true. But, honestly, I didn't have the courage. When I got there, I couldn't go through with it. Pathetic, I know. Pathetic."

That was it, thought Dykeman, the man had lost hope. You could hear it in his voice, as well as see it in his eyes. Maybe he was telling the truth. Maybe.

"What did you do then, if you didn't follow Graball into that room?"

"The young woman I'd seen from the top floor came back through the doors from reception. She looked confused, uncertain you could say. I asked her if I could walk her back to the function room. That was it. I don't think either of us said anything after that. I know I didn't. I was too pre-occupied with my own thoughts."

"And this young woman, how would you describe her emotional state?"

Plenty thought for a moment before answering. "Agitated. She looked unhappy and confused."

"You don't know why that might have been?"

"No."

"And that's it. The two of you walked off together and didn't have anything else to do with Henry Graball?"

"Listen, inspector. I know I shouldn't have lied to you. I was an idiot to do that. But I never even spoke to Henry and...

I doubt I'd have the guts to kill a man, no matter how tight a spot I was in."

Dykeman eyed Plenty with suspicion. The man had wobbled, but he hadn't collapsed. Whoever it was that killed Graball, they would have needed time to dispose of the knife and that coat, without being seen. Did Plenty or Slip have such an opportunity before they bumped into each other? Plenty had at least admitted Wendy Slip wasn't there when he arrived outside the room, but had there been enough time for him to go into that room, murder Graball, make it over to the cloakroom and then be back in the hallway before Slip returned? Or could Slip have done the same before Plenty arrived on the scene? Or was Graball still alive when the two of them left him to it? Still so many questions to be answered.

"You're quite right, Mr Plenty. You shouldn't have lied to us. Put you in a very bad light, that has. I would suggest you tread very carefully from here on in and make sure there's no repeat of that sort of thing. We're done with you for now, but you should understand you're an undoubted suspect in this case and I would expect we'll want to speak to you again, so make sure you don't go far."

"That's fair enough, Inspector. I was a fool and you can rest assured that sort of thing won't happen again. If there's anything I can do, you've only to ask. Anything."

Dykeman and Shapes left Plenty visibly relieved, resting his head up against the wall of the house. The Inspector, on the other hand, was feeling a little disappointed. He'd thought they were close to identifying the killer, especially when Plenty seemed about to crumble under his relentless questioning. Now he wasn't entirely sure they'd made any real progress at all. It felt more like they had missed an opportunity. He batted away the thought. They were, he reminded himself, making progress; one step at a time, as they always did.

"Thought we had him there, Shapes."

"Me too, sir. Could still be he's guilty, though. Wouldn't trust a word he says."

"Yes, thought he was about to cave in. Don't know about Plenty. Part of me says he did it and part says he didn't. There's more work to be done there before we can be sure either way. Still, we shouldn't lose sight of the fact things are looking up. People have been lying to us, Shapes, and when they do that it usually means they've got something to hide. All we need to do, Shapes, is work out which one of 'em is trying to hide the fact they're a killer."

Shapes had been mightily impressed with his boss's performance when questioning Plenty. Wouldn't have thought he had it in him to be so merciless. Normally he was way too soft. Perhaps his own hard-nosed approach was finally starting to rub off on Dykeman.

As they arrived back at the car, Shapes felt a moment's disappointment at the prospect of leaving the building site so soon. Perhaps there'd be an unexpected need for him to return some other time. He could always hope.

Chapter Eleven

Daphne Graball was sitting in the living room of her home, looking fondly at the chair where she had so often watched the figure of her sleeping husband. He always preferred to sit in the high-backed armchair by the fire. It never made any difference whether the fire was lit or not; he'd walk into the house in the evening, greet her with a tender kiss on the cheek, then make his way through to the living room as soon as he possibly could. He'd let out a deep sigh of contentment as he slumped on to the chair and close his eyes for a moment or two. She could almost see the stress lift from his shoulders.

He liked to have a cup of tea before they ate. He said it helped settle him down. She would take it through to him and tell him to relax while she finished preparing their dinner. It always had been hard to understand why so many other people thought Henry to be such an unpleasant and disagreeable man. Perhaps these people ought to visit them at home; then they'd see what a wonderful man he really was. He'd always been good to her, loving and caring, as much as any man could be when you considered how little time he got to spend at home. And she had never wanted for anything. Life had been everything she had ever dreamed of. She had loved him deeply, almost from the moment they met, and she always would.

At least, that had been her view of her husband and their relationship until recently. She'd started to hear unsettling things about Henry. She might have been able to ignore them if it had just been one or two people who'd been involved, but it wasn't. A number of her friends had said odd things to her. Whatever it was they wanted to say, they never seemed able to come right out with it and would, instead, drop peculiar comments into conversations with her.

She had started to look at him differently. Wondered where he spent his time when he was away from home and if there were places he went and people he spent time with that had nothing to do with business. Everything he had ever done outside of their home had revolved around making money. Even when he was at home, his mind was often elsewhere. There were phone calls and visitors. He never really let go, at least not for very long.

The nagging doubts had begun to eat away at her. Some mornings she'd watch him drive away from the house and feel so terribly lonely. Then the loneliness was joined by fear and a terrible sense of being inadequate, not enough for the man she loved.

Then she found out about Wendy Slip. An anonymous note from a 'well-wisher' concerned about the way her husband was treating her. She was certain it was a man. She couldn't imagine a woman writing such a thing in so matter-of-fact way. They even told her where to find the two lovers every Thursday evening. So she took the train to Oxford and waited in the shadows across the road from the Little Venice restaurant, shaking with trepidation.

They arrived in a taxi, at the hour she had been told they would, and they walked into the restaurant arm-in-arm. A tear ran down her cheek as she watched the door close behind them. She nearly left there and then, but something held her back, persuaded her to stay until they left. When they did, she saw them embrace in the back of the taxi and kiss, long and passionately.

Even before she'd arrived back in Banbury, the shock and tears had already been replaced by anger and determination. If Henry imagined for one moment he could carry on like that, without her lifting a finger in response, then he really was a very foolish man indeed.

"Daphne, dear, did you hear me?"

The voice of Anne Nettle interrupted her thoughts and she felt a little confused for a moment as she brought herself back to the here and now.

"I'm sorry Anne, dear. I find it so hard to concentrate at the moment. What was it you said?"

"Oh, you don't need to apologise, Daphne. Good Lord, you've every reason to find things difficult. I'm not so sure I would be able to cope half as well as you have if anything of the sort befell Nigel. Probably end up a complete and utter wreck. I was just asking who it is that's taking care of Henry's business interests. Only I hope no one is bothering you with such things. It really wouldn't be right for them to expect you to involve yourself in such things now. Though I suppose someone has to take care of it all."

Anne Nettle paused to pick up her cup of tea. Daphne Graball managed a feeble smile, barely moving the corners of her mouth.

"It's good of you to be concerned, Anne, but I think the office can manage on their own for a while."

"I don't suppose either of the children are likely to step up to the plate, are they? They've not shown any interest up to now, I mean. Would be quite a surprise if they changed their minds, even if it would mean you could forget all about such things."

"No, I doubt very much they will want to get involved. I think they are intent on doing other things with their lives."

Anne Nettle opened her mouth to speak again, but at that precise moment the chimes of the doorbell filled the air.

"Now just you wait there, Daphne. I'll see to that. Probably one of those door-to-door salesmen that have been swarming all over town lately. I'll soon have them on their way, don't you worry about that. Had to chase one of them down our garden path only last week. Horrid man."

Daphne Graball let out a little sigh as her friend disappeared into the hallway. If truth be told, she really would prefer to be left alone, but she knew that it was probably good for her to spend some time in other people's company. She would just drop deeper into despondency otherwise. Oh, what had she done with her life all these years? Everything she ever did seemed to revolve around Henry and now he was gone things seemed so... empty. There was nothing there for her. It was a thought that caused a little bubble of resentment to rise inside her.

"Daphne, dear, it's the police. They want to speak to you. Shall I let them in? I can always tell them to go away if you'd rather not talk to them at the moment. They've no right to be pestering you like this. They really ought to know better."

"It's alright, Anne. Let them in."

As Anne Nettle made her way back to the front door, Daphne Graball felt overwhelmed by anxiety; a deep-seated worry as to why the police wanted to speak to her. For three days, her nerves had been eating away at her, leaving her restless and on-edge during the day and hardly able to sleep at night. Perhaps they wouldn't stay long. A few minutes with them wouldn't be so bad. She could hold herself together for as long as that.

Dykeman had been a little surprised to encounter Anne Nettle at the Graballs's home. The woman seemed to get everywhere. That is, everywhere he and Shapes went. Coincidences were not something to set any store by, as far as he was concerned, so finding the woman here with Daphne Graball after bumping into her at the Louches home was borderline suspicious. And acting like some kind of border guard, holding them back from entering the premises, what was that all about? He watched her large bottom wobble its way along the hall, wondering if they shouldn't be asking her some questions after they'd spoken to Daphne Graball.

"Here we are, Daphne dear. It's Inspector Dykeman and Sergeant Sharps. Are you sure you're up to talking to them?"

Daphne Graball nodded her head, then stood up to greet the two policemen.

"Hello Inspector. Sergeant Shapes. Would you like to sit down."

"Thank you, Mrs Graball," replied Dykeman before turning to his sergeant. "Shapes, if you wouldn't mind seeing Mrs Nettle off the premises. This needs to be a private conversation."

"Oh... I can always wait in the dining room, or perhaps..."

Anne Nettle was still putting up a fight as Shapes steered her away, towards the front door. He didn't exactly fling her out the building, but nor did he put up with any attempted lingering. The smile on his face as he closed the door was entirely genuine. It was bad enough she'd got his name wrong, but neither he nor Dykeman cared much for people who tried to stick their nose in where it was not wanted.

"How are you doing, Mrs Graball? Still feeling upset I shouldn't imagine?"

"My doctor tells me it's the shock, Inspector. He wanted to put me on medication, but I don't want to block the world out. That wouldn't be right. I suppose things will heal with time."

He'd had to become immune to the suffering people felt in such situations, otherwise not only would he be unable to do his job properly, he would also be likely to have a total breakdown, sooner or later. Having too much sympathy for people like Daphne Graball was a dangerous thing to do. Worse still, her situation brought back painful memories of his own father's death. He allowed the recollection to linger briefly, tempted for a moment to let it wash right over him, then pushed it to the back of his mind, where it could wait for a more appropriate time. Such things were best re-visited when you had the benefit of privacy, he always thought.

"Time the healer? That's what they say and I guess there's some truth in that. That woman gone, Shapes?"

"Not without a fight, sir. Probably hiding by the window now, hoping she can hear a word or two."

Shapes sat down on an enormous settee next to Dykeman. The thing was so big it would take up all of the space in his own living room. He fished out his notepad and pencil.

"Anne doesn't mean any harm," smiled Daphne Graball. "She's been wonderful since... the other day."

Glad to hear Shapes confirm that Anne Nettle was off the premises, Dykeman decided to get down to business.

"We hear you made a trip down to Oxford yesterday, Mrs Graball."

"Oh, you've heard about that," she replied, sounding a little contrite. "I feel so foolish now, losing my temper like that. But, under the circumstances... I was just so angry, Inspector. I don't know if it was the shock of finding out Henry had been seeing another woman or anger at myself for... Did that young man put in a complaint?"

"He did indeed."

"He was very good, you know. Barely more than a boy and he had to put himself right between the two of us. He looked rather nervous. Probably thought we might both start hitting him."

Daphne Graball managed to sound a little amused and her eyes came to life. Dykeman thought perhaps they'd had a brief glimpse of the woman she was before her husband had been murdered.

"Think I would have been a bit worried myself, Mrs Graball. Very public-spirited of him."

"I was so angry with her, you understand. Furious. She knew, of course, that Henry was married. I suppose she didn't mind that if it meant she got to live rent-free in that nice flat. And all the clothes, the jewellery and perfume and everything else. I don't know what I would have done if that young man hadn't intervened. You might have been asked to place me under arrest, Inspector. "

"I can imagine it was very hard on you, finding out your husband had been unfaithful, especially after what had happened already."

"I felt so foolish. My husband doing something like that."

She trailed off, not sure what to say next.

"It might not be much of a help, but there's plenty more been down that road before you and, sad to say, there'll be a whole load more after you. Seems to be the way of things."

"The thing is, Inspector, on the train journey back home, I started to feel sorry for the young woman. I think I began to see that she, too, was deeply upset by Henry's death and, whilst I can't forgive her, I also can't stop myself from acknowledging her pain. And it wasn't as if she was the only one involved in the relationship. Henry has to take just as much blame as her."

"That's very understanding of you, Mrs Graball. I think a lesser person wouldn't be half as considerate as that."

"You think your life is so secure and certain, Inspector, then something happens that you could never expect and things begin to unravel so quickly you find it hard to keep up. I hardly know what to think any more."

"You have two adult children, don't you? Are they on their way here?"

She nodded, her shoulders slumped now and any hint of happiness gone from her voice once more.

"They will be here this evening. I will be so glad to see them."

"That's good. There was one other thing I wondered whether you might be able to help us with, Mrs Graball. Your husband made a loan to a local architect, Owen Plenty. Did he say anything to you about that?"

"Owen Plenty? Oh, yes. Henry did mention him once or twice. I think they first met quite some time ago. But Henry never said anything about lending money to Mr Plenty. Was it a very substantial loan?"

"Well, it was by mine and Shapes's standards. Maybe not so big as far as your husband was concerned. I think it's fair to say it's a pretty big loan in Owen Plenty's eyes. Your husband never said anything at all about it?"

"No, I'm sure about that. But Henry wasn't in the habit of discussing business with me. I think he knew it rather bored me. You could try speaking to his accountant."

"We've done that already, but I think your husband played his cards pretty close to his chest. Well, thank you Mrs Graball. We'll leave you in peace now."

Daphne Graball came to life in an instant, her eyes wide open and a pleading hand held up in front of her.

"Oh, but Inspector, you haven't told me how your investigation is going. Are you close to finding the killer?"

Dykeman had hoped to duck that one, knowing he couldn't go sharing any particulars with the widow, but at the same time not wanting it to look like he and Shapes were inept and nowhere near making an arrest. Relatives in these cases always thought the police should have the guilty party under lock and key in two shakes of a lamb's tale. Twenty-four hours was about the limit. Get beyond that and the questions started landing ever thicker and ever faster, until it got to the point where you were doing your best to avoid the frustrated relatives, who were, at the same time, doing their utmost to corner you. Best to leave Mrs Graball with an optimistic view of things, without actually committing to anything he could be held to. Mind you, that was easier said than done.

"Well, you understand we can't go telling you any particulars, Mrs Graball, not while the case is still in progress. But I can say that Shapes and I have made some solid progress, maybe even a bit more than I might have expected by now. There were a lot of people in that building at the time of your husband's murder. Huge number of statements to be taken and analysed. But we've narrowed things down very satisfactorily, wouldn't you say, Shapes."

"Been going very nicely, sir. Like you say, solid progress."

Git, thought Shapes. Dykeman putting him on the spot like that. Say the wrong thing and before you know it you're being hauled before a disciplinary, having to explain yourself. He wasn't taking any chances there. If Dykeman wanted him to say something, then all he was going to do was repeat anything his boss had already said. They'd have words about that later.

"That's so good to hear, Inspector. I'm sure it can't be an easy thing to do, speaking to so many people and trying work out who might be lying to you and who is telling the truth. It's just the thought that whoever did kill Henry might get away with it. I couldn't bear that."

Daphne Graball's voice fell away to a whisper and her eyes lost the energy they had displayed for a brief while.

"Don't you going worrying about that, Mrs Graball. Shapes and I won't let up until we've got 'em."

THE GRABALL RESIDENCE was quiet as the two officers stepped out on to the driveway. Even the passing traffic seemed to have pretty much dried up and all they could hear was the happy chirping of birds coming from a small group of trees in one corner of the front garden. Shapes scratched the side of his face, where stubble was beginning to darken the flesh, and looked at his boss.

"You think she could have done it, sir?"

Although Dykeman had a ready enough answer to the question, he took a moment to consider things. Was he being too quick to make a judgement or was he right to trust to his instinct? It was hard to tell. There were as many reasons to consider the widow guilty as there to think her innocent, but, as of now, he found himself leaning in one direction.

"I do, Shapes. Indeed I do."

Chapter Twelve

Dykeman sat behind his desk, picking at his teeth where bits of the toast he'd eaten for breakfast had got stuck. He was restless. Shapes's question outside the Graballs's house had been playing on his mind most of the night. Up until then he hadn't properly considered the possibility that Daphne Graball might have murdered her husband. She had seemed too genuinely upset and, despite everything they had found out about him, very much in love with her husband. But there was no getting away from the fact she had a rock solid motive in the shape of her husband's extra-marital affairs and there were plenty of people who had resorted to murder in such circumstances.

Perhaps they ought to go back through all those witness statements, looking to see if Daphne Graball had an opportunity to do the deed. It hadn't looked like it before, but then they hadn't been keeping an eye out for that. They'd probably made a mistake there. Made an assumption, which was never a good thing to do. Damn it, this new uncertainty was clouding his mind.

Shapes ambled into the room, rolled up newspaper under one arm, a mug of something steaming in one hand and a plate with a sandwich on it in the other.

"You got the Racing Post there, Shapes?"

"Certainly have, sir."

"How'd we do yesterday? Pick up some tasty winnings?"

"Afraid not. Came in second, by half-a-length. French Kiss came in first."

"Damn it. I thought we were on to a winner there. Where'd your tip come from?"

"Stable lad at Towcester. He's got a brother works at Houghton's yard. Horse must have got out the wrong side of bed."

"What about today? Anything we can make our money back on?"

"There's two I like the look of. Pretty Pete goes in the three-thirty at Wolverhampton. Five-to-one. Came second to Hairy Helen last time out. Or there's Tall Tales in the one-forty-five at Newmarket. Small field. Three-to-one looks pretty good to me."

"Go on then, I'll have a quid on each one. Now then, I want to go back through all the statements today. I think we might have missed a trick."

"Daphne Graball?" asked Shapes, dropping the Racing Post on his desk.

"Yes, worried we might have slipped up there."

"Thinking it might be the obvious one?"

"Revenge?" answered Dykeman.

Shapes nodded as he placed his mug of coffee on his desk.

"Would look pretty stupid if it did turn out to be her and we hadn't bothered looking into the possibility by now. If it is her, then she's been doing a damn good job of appearing to be upset." continued Dykeman.

"She's a woman, sir. What do you expect?"

"Yes, Shapes, she's a woman. I had noticed."

"What about that Nettle woman? You noticed how she keeps popping up here, there and everywhere? Bloody suspicious, if you ask me."

"I had noticed, Shapes. Maybe she's just plain nosy. Let's keep her on our reserve list for now."

"Reserve list?"

"That's right. The one we fall back on if we can't find anything to pin on our prime suspects. Always a good idea to have a fall-back position, Shapes. You should know that."

"Sounds a bit desperate to me."

The phone on Dykeman's desk interrupted their conversation. The inspector answered it.

"Dykeman."

There was a short pause as the inspector listened to what was being said. His left eyebrow arched upwards.

"Missing, you say? Do we have a home address? Just a moment."

Dykeman dug a pencil and paper out of one of the desk drawers and scribbled down an address.

"Yes, we'll get right over there. Thank you."

"Something happened, has it, sir?" asked Shapes, through a mouthful of bacon, gherkin and bread.

"It's Tinkler, the waiter seen arguing with Henry Graball. He's not shown up for work. Should have been there at eight this morning. The general manager at the Conservative Club just phoned it through, thinking we might be interested. Good man."

"Well, that's a turn-up for the books. We going round to his house?"

"Seems to me to be as good a place as any to start looking for him. Don't suppose you've had a chance to check out Tinkler yet?"

"It's on my to-do list for this morning. You want me to make a start on it now?"

"No, let's focus on trying to find him. Get one of the uniformed mob to do some digging while we're gone."

"I'll have a word with Dartington. I saw him in the canteen with his feet up, reading the newspaper. I reckon he needs something to do."

"Good. I'll meet you in the car park. I need to spend a penny before we leave."

SYDNEY TINKLER RENTED a two-up two-down Victorian house on Queen's Road, not far from the centre of town. It took the two policemen fewer than five minutes to drive there. From the pavement outside, Dykeman looked up at number seventeen with a degree of disapproval. The house was run down almost to the point of being dilapidated. Long strips of white paint were peeling from every window frame, the down-pipe from the guttering had partially come away up by one of the bedroom windows and much of the pointing needed re-doing.

"Bit of a dive," observed Shapes, from the other side of the car.

Dykeman looked round at the neighbouring properties, none of which were in as bad a state, even if they weren't the most upmarket of places. Most likely an absent landlord, who pocketed the money collected by an agent, but had no interest in spending anything on maintenance.

"Reminds me of your bathroom, Shapes."

"My bathroom? I'll have you know I cleaned that at the weekend. It's spotless. Almost."

"If you say so, Shapes."

They walked up the short path of rectangular red tiles, most of which were either cracked or had bits missing, and stopped in front of a door with a misted glass panel in its top half. Shapes raised a fist and hammered three times on the wooden frame. The door moved visibly, the lock not holding it securely in place. There was no response. Shapes knocked again, while Dykeman stepped into the small, weed-infested garden and tried to peer in through the bay window.

"Can't see a damn thing with these net curtains up," complained the Inspector. "Just shadows."

"We could have a look round the back," suggested Shapes, trying to see through the frosted window in the door, also without any success.

"Might as well."

They found a partially-slabbed pathway at the top end of the street that led round to the back of the houses on their side of the street and, counting their way as they went, navigated their way to number seventeen. There was a small, mess-strewn yard and an old outside toilet that appeared to still be in use, the stink getting right up the nose of both men, much to their disgust.

Dykeman tried looking in through the single tall, dirty window, but once again the standard issue net curtains put paid to that. Shapes made straight for the door, which was struggling to cling on to the last vestiges of the dark green paint which had once covered its timbers. As he turned the handle, the door eased open.

"We're in luck, sir. Door's not locked."

"Well done, Shapes. On we go, then."

They found themselves entering a narrow kitchen, the light from the open doorway falling on a dirt and grease-coated floor. Shapes stepped across to the small, ancient stove and gingerly felt the side of the kettle that sat on one of the two gas rings. It was stone cold. No one had been making tea there for at least the last couple of hours. He turned back towards Dykeman and, without saying a word, shook his head.

A hallway led off the rear of the kitchen, dark and musty. Dykeman ran a finger over the nearest wall and found it as greasy as the walls in the room they'd just left. It was obvious, Tinkler wasn't a man for doing the housework. Halfway down on their right were two adjacent doors, both closed, and just beyond that, on the left, the stairs doubled back and up to the first floor. Dykeman shivered, realising the temperature had dropped like a stone since they'd entered the house, despite the time of year.

Shapes opened the first of the doors and the two of them stepped into a modest-sized room, typical of that sort of house.

It was empty, aside from a pair of battered wooden chairs that sat up against one of the walls. Dirty, flower-patterned wallpaper peeled away in sections up by the ceiling and the fireplace grate had been boarded over. The two men looked at each other, then left the room without exchanging a word.

Shapes had to give the second door a bit of a shove to get it open, the top corner sticking hard against the frame, and he tumbled into the room as it gave way. Dykeman noticed the light switch on the wall by the door and flicked it on. A low wattage bulb hanging naked from the ceiling sparked into life, lifting the gloom. The room stunk to high heaven of cigarettes, causing both men to cough.

Shapes, having regained his balance and composure, looked down at the middle of the floor and shook his head. Dykeman's view was obscured at first by a high-backed armchair and he had to take another step into the room before he could see what had caught his sergeant's attention. There, on the worn and dirty carpet, was the body of a man, face down, arms spread out to the sides and his thinning grey hair stained dark red.

Taking care not to step on anything that might turn out to be a clue, Shapes went round the far side of the body and peered down at the exposed face.

"It's him, sir. Sydney Tinkler."

"Pulse?" asked Dykeman, more in hope than expectation.

Shapes squatted down and felt at Tinkler's right wrist and then the matching temple. He wasn't an expert at that sort of thing, he'd readily admit to anyone who might ask, but he was damned if he could detect a pulse. The man was a goner.

"Nope. He's dead as they come." He took a close look through the matted hair at the back of the skull. "Looks like he's been smashed over the head. Nasty." He looked again. "My money's on a hammer."

Dykeman looked around him, but there was no sign of a murder weapon. They might get lucky and find that later, once they had a team on site to carry out a proper search. He took another look around the room, careful to make a mental note of whatever was there and to consider if anything he saw might be a clue as to what had happened and who else had been there. But there was nothing that might help.

In fact, there wasn't much at all. There was a second armchair over by the window, a low rectangular table on which was a discarded jumble of newspapers, a couple of books and an almost empty pint glass. There was a second small table on the other side of the chair Dykeman had been standing beside. On top of that stood a modern radio. As his eyes moved further around the room, the Inspector noticed the fireplace.

"Check that out, will you, Shapes."

The sergeant held a hand over the faded embers, moving it lower and lower, until he'd satisfied himself.

"Still a bit of heat there. Not much, but some. Probably went out a couple of hours ago."

"That blood looks pretty dry, too. I'm guessing he was done in last night some time." Dykeman puffed his cheeks and scratched the back of his head. "But is it connected to Henry Graball's murder? That's the question I'd like an answer to most of all."

"Bit of a coincidence if it isn't."

"You're probably right, Shapes, but we'd best not go making any assumptions. Don't suppose you've noticed a phone here?"

Shapes shook his head. "Don't look like he's got one."

"You'd best get back to the station and round up some troops. Let Sheila Delph know, too. See if she can get down here right away. Would be good to get a better idea of time of death. And another thing: get someone to find out what our suspects were doing last night. Matthew Louch, Owen Plenty and Wendy Slip. And I'm looking for proper alibis."

"What about Daphne Graball? Not going to leave her out, are we?"

"I suppose not. Yes, add her to the list. I'm going to wait here with the body." He took another look at Sydney Tinkler's corpse. "Might as well take a look upstairs while I'm about it. Well, off you go then. And be quick about it."

WITH HIS SERGEANT GONE, Dykeman felt distinctly uncomfortable, alone with the body of Tinkler in the cold, run-down, filthy house. He felt a shiver run up his spine, as if someone, or something, was watching him. He thought perhaps a cup of tea would help calm his unease, but the sight of the grime in the kitchen put him off that idea straight away. Talk about a public health hazard. How had Tinkler put up with living in such a place? Did his job at the Conservative Club really pay him that badly?

Not keen on remaining in the same room as the corpse, Dykeman risked a trip up the stairs, feeling he really ought to take a look in the remaining rooms. Just like the rest of the house, the two bedrooms were cold and gloomy, clearly not having been re-decorated in many years. The back bedroom was entirely empty. The front bedroom, on the other hand, contained a single, unmade bed, a small wardrobe and a chest of drawers, all of which looked Victorian.

With considerable reluctance, Dykeman nudged open the wardrobe door, to be met by the almost over-powering stink of moth balls. He leaned back, waved a hand in front of his face, to no real effect, then girded his loins and peered into the dark recesses of the wardrobe. To his surprise, there were two clean and ironed white shirts, along with a pair of equally clean and well-pressed navy trousers on hangers. They looked so out of place in the house that Dykeman wondered for a moment if he wasn't experiencing some sort of hallucination and reached out with a hand to make certain they were really there. Then it occurred to him that Tinkler wouldn't last long working at the Conservative Club if he showed up dressed like a tramp.

Having completed his inspection of the wardrobe, the Inspector moved on to the chest of drawers. They too contained impressively clean items of clothing, socks, underwear, vests and even a pair of black leather gloves. And that was it. Talk about Spartan, mused Dykeman. The man could get his entire wardrobe of clothes into a single modest-sized suitcase, something Dykeman doubted very much he could do himself. To Dykeman's mind, that suggested Tinkler viewed his current, and, as it turned out, final domestic arrangements as being temporary in nature. Surely to God, someone who planned on remaining in a place for a decent stretch of time would own more things than Tinkler did.

There was no separate bathroom. Given the state of the property it was hardly surprising, thought Dykeman. Tinkler must have washed in the kitchen, decided Dykeman, just like they did when he was a kid and his mum would dunk him in an old tin bath filled with hot water in the middle of the kitchen. That had been a once-a-week affair he always looked forward to.

Back downstairs, trying hard not to succumb to the lingering feelings of unease he felt as he returned to the living room, Dykeman gave some thought to why Tinkler might have been killed. He found it hard, almost impossible, not to imagine that it was in some way or another connected to the murder of Henry Graball. He didn't much care for coincidences; they were all too often an excuse to avoid hard work and difficult problems.

But if it did have something to do with Graball, what might that something be? Could he have been Graball's killer? Had Daphne Graball somehow found this out, then taken her own gory revenge? Or what if he had been paid to murder Henry Graball and his paymaster had then decided not to leave any loose ends hanging around? Or had Graball employed Tinkler on some sinister deed, the victim of which had taken such exception they'd struck out at the two of them? The problem was, as things stood, there just weren't any clues, not even weak ones, as to what the connection was. Well, maybe something would show up in the report his officers were putting together on Tinkler. He could but hope.

Just when Dykeman was beginning to seriously think he might prefer to wait outside the house, away from Tinkler's corpse and that persistent feeling of unease, he heard the familiar wail of a siren in the street outside, followed moments later by noise of a car jolting to a halt. Walking down the hallway and opening the front door, he saw Shapes and two uniformed officers climbing out of their vehicle. Within seconds there was another patrol car parked behind the first and the whole street seemed to be filled with uniforms.

"Any luck with Delph?" he asked Shapes, as his sergeant approached the house.

"Should be here shortly. Said she wondered what had been keeping us. It's been days since we had a body for her to inspect."

"Well, we wouldn't want her to go without work, would we now? I've nosed around upstairs. Nothing. The man owned two shirts, a pair of trousers and half-a-dozen pairs of sock and Y-fronts. Not exactly the lap of luxury."

"No weapon, then?"

"Sadly not."

"I've given this lot their orders," said Shapes, waving a hand in the general direction of the uniformed officers who were dispersing along the road. "I've got half of them going door-to-door and the rest doing a search for whatever it was the killer used to smash in Tinkler's head. If they dumped it round here somewhere, we'll find it."

"Good work, Shapes. I don't suppose that background check on Tinkler's been done?"

"Not all of it, sir. But we've got a few bits and bobs and there's something very interesting."

Dykeman had been watching one of the constables as he rapped on the door of a house opposite. As Shapes finished speaking, his attention swung back to his sergeant, expectation thick on the air.

"Well, get on with it. What's so bloody interesting?"

Shapes coughed. "He's a crook. Well, I say a crook. Should really say he's a suspected crook."

"What do you mean 'suspected'?"

"His last job, before he moved here, was at a members club in Manchester. Same sort of work as he did here. Seems money kept going missing from the club coffers and every time it happened Tinkler had been there or thereabouts. Dead certain were the Manchester police that he was responsible, but they could never pin it on him."

"Sticky fingers, eh? Well, if he was helping himself to their funds, God knows what he was doing with it. There's nothing to show for it here. Did they sack him?"

"There was an incident with one of the waitresses. She complained and the club took their chance. Kicked him out there and then."

"And he decided to move well away. Makes sense."

"But that's not all." Shapes's voice had acquired an air of superiority, suggesting he hadn't yet landed the juiciest piece of news at his disposal.

Dykeman looked in expectation at his sergeant, who remained silent.

"You're like a young child sometimes, Shapes, do you know that? And what is the most important thing you've found out?"

"Guess who was a guest at the club in Manchester, several times?"

"The Pope?"

"Nope."

"Shapes!" Dykeman was getting annoyed.

"Henry Graball."

Chapter Thirteen

The news from Shapes had left Dykeman temporarily open-mouthed. What a development. Graball and Tinkler very likely knew each other before the now deceased waiter moved south. Once again, Dykeman found himself dismissing the notion of coincidence. That was for the lazy and incompetent, of which he was certain he was neither, despite the opinions of one or two people who bore him a grudge.

However, before Dykeman had an opportunity to debate the matter with his sergeant, Sheila Delph, the pathologist for the north of the county, hove into view, apparently having walked to the house; at least, there was no sign of her car.

"Ah, Sheila, you're here already," said Dykeman, as the pathologist turned on to the small path in front of the house. "Wonderful."

"Good morning, Leslie. I understand you have some work for me."

Delph's eyes sparkled, at least as far as Dykeman was concerned. And her voice had a soft, velvety quality he found both irresistible and disconcerting. She was wearing a dark green, two-piece skirt and jacket outfit that made her look... Dykeman struggled to put his finger on it. It made her look what precisely? Best not dwell on that any longer, he decided.

"Indeed we do. One Sydney Tinkler. He's been whacked over the head. He's on the floor in the living room." Dykeman glanced up the street again. "You walk here, did you?"

"I do have legs, Leslie. In case you hadn't noticed."

"Indeed." Dykeman felt a warm glow rise in his cheeks and hoped he hadn't reddened enough for the other two to notice.

"I suppose you drove?"

Dykeman wasn't entirely clear if that was a question or an accusation. "It's Shapes. He won't walk anywhere. Surprised he can make it down to the staff canteen and back."

Shapes shook his head but maintained his silence.

"This way?" asked Delph.

"Yes, I'll show you."

"Does this have anything to do with Henry Graball's murder?" asked Delph as they entered the house. "Or shouldn't I ask?"

"Oh, you can ask whatever you like," replied Dykeman. "We've nothing yet that connects the two murders for certain, but you know me, I don't do coincidences. Just found out from Shapes that the two men very likely knew each other before Tinkler moved to Banbury from Manchester."

"Well, let's see what I can do for you."

The two policemen watched in silence as Delph got down to business. Shapes was fascinated by her work and had even once managed to persuade her to let him watch as she performed a postmortem. True enough, he had needed to shut his eyes at one point, when things got really gory, but he had stood there, transfixed as she went about things, giving him a running commentary as she went. If he'd had the brains, he might have been tempted to give up police work and train to become a doctor, so he too could chop people up. The nearest he'd ever got to that sort of thing was dissecting grasshoppers on his dad's allotment when he was thirteen or fourteen years old.

It didn't take Delph more than five minutes to carry out her initial inspection of Tinkler. The cause of death looked clear and, as far as she could tell, there was nothing else that appeared suspicious.

"Well," she announced, getting back to her feet. "All the usual caveats apply, of course, but the cause of death seems to be very clear. He's been hit over the head with a blunt instrument of some sort. There are at least two blows, very close together, and the worst of them was probably enough to cause death. In my opinion, he was hit from behind. I can't see anything else of interest, but I'll need to carry out a full examination before I can be certain about that."

"Would it have needed a lot of force to do enough damage to kill him? What I mean is, could a woman have done it?" asked the Inspector.

"If they used a hammer or something similar, then I'm sure a woman would be capable of hitting him hard enough; though whoever it was would have needed to swing their arm fully extended, I should imagine."

Dykeman was silent for a moment, chewing on his bottom lip. Delph knew him well enough to perceive something was on his mind and she waited patiently for him to work out what he wanted to say.

"Do you think it's possible that whoever did this might find it believable if they heard Tinkler wasn't dead?"

Delph looked at the policeman with a quizzical expression on her face. "What on earth do you mean, Leslie?"

"I've got an idea. I think we might be able to use what's happened here to flush out the killer."

It was only as he spoke the words that Dykeman truly began to believe what he had in mind was possible and just might work. But he wanted Delph's opinion first. She was the sensible sort and wouldn't hold back from telling him if she thought he was being idiotic.

"Really?" Delph sounded perplexed. "Well, I suppose if the killer has never had any medical training it might sound plausible. But don't you imagine they would have checked to make sure he was dead?"

Shapes was nodding his head and looking at his boss sideways, every bit as confused and curious as Delph.

"That's the point. If you're a trained doctor or nurse, you can be sure you've got it right. There wouldn't be any doubt in your mind that Tinkler is dead. But what if you're not? What if you think you've checked properly but you can't be absolutely certain. If you then read in the newspaper that Tinkler has, by some miracle, survived, could you really just sit there telling yourself he was dead?"

"You want to use him as bait," suggested a smiling Shapes.

Dykeman nodded. "That's right. Put word out Tinkler has survived. Maybe say he's in a coma, receiving the best medical attention, and the doctor's are confident he'll pull through.

Add that we fully expect him to be able to tell us who attacked him."

"Oh," declared Delph. "And then you hope the killer will have another go?"

"Exactly." Dykeman gave a little sideways shake of the head and smacked his lips together. "What do you think?"

"It could work," replied Delph, more than a hint of admiration in her voice. It really was an impressively imaginative scheme. Not, she thought to herself, the kind of thing she would normally expect from Dykeman.

"Don't see how the killer could resist," added Shapes. "They'd have to think their days were numbered if Tinkler was expected to recover. I'd have another go."

"I know you would, Shapes. You'd probably consider it a matter of personal pride to make sure the job got done properly. Well, let's give it a go, then. I don't suppose we've got anything to lose."

"Oh, how exciting," announced Delph. "I'll arrange for an ambulance to collect Tinkler and I can speak to my colleagues at the hospital about the arrangements there, if you're happy for me to do that, Leslie?"

"I'll take whatever help you can offer, Sheila. That will leave me and Shapes to set up a little press briefing. And this is going to be one meeting with the press boys I actually don't mind attending."

DYKEMAN HAD DECIDED he really couldn't afford not to seek the permission of the Chief Inspector for his cunning little scheme. It was something he would have preferred not to do, but to his complete surprise he received nothing but encouragement. Mind you, this was on the understanding that if things went badly he would be the one to carry the can. Nothing new there, Dykeman mused.

With the level of interest that already existed around the town and its environs for the investigation into Graball's murder, it took no serious encouragement for reporters from across the county to make their way to Banbury police station, especially once it was made clear there had been an attempt at a second murder, believed to be related to Graball's killing.

The modest-sized room they used for meetings with the press was very nearly full, with a mixture of reporters and photographers national and local, who possessed a level of bright-eyed interest Dykeman found a little disconcerting. But he put that to one side, delighted at the size of the turn-out. All he needed to do now was put on his usual bumbling performance on such occasions, so as to avoid the risk of arousing suspicion, and let the press get to work on his behalf.

Dykeman did his best to appear both uncomfortable and incompetent. Since he'd managed this on numerous previous occasions without intending to, it didn't exactly take a lot of effort.

Questions fell upon him in sudden flurries and he felt he did a good job at answering them as unhelpfully as possible. This belief seemed to be confirmed in a most pleasing manner by the occasional grunt or groan from the room.

All the same, by the time he brought proceedings to an end, there was no doubt at all in his mind that he'd got his message across. The various representatives of the press were up and heading for the exit, full of excitement, like little school children off on a nature trip.

"Bloody good job that, sir. You had them eating out of the palm of your hand," congratulated Shapes, as soon as the room had emptied.

"Thank you, Shapes. Yes, it did go well. Shame the Chief Inspector wasn't here to see it."

"They won't be happy, mind."

"Who?"

"That lot," replied Shapes, nodding in the direction of the departing reporters. "They won't like the fact they've been played for a bunch of idiots, even if that's what they are."

"Tough." Dykeman thought about it a bit more. "I'll butter them up. Tell them we couldn't have done it all without them."

"We couldn't."

"Well, there you go, then. Now, let's get over to the hospital and see how they've been getting on."

Chapter Fourteen

The first report of their press briefing was included with the one o'clock news on the BBC Home Service. Shapes and Dykeman were sitting in the palatial office of the hospital general manager, listening to his radio, fingers crossed. They couldn't be certain the BBC would pick up the story and the pair of them nodded with satisfaction as the news announcer worked his way through the report. All the key points were there. The attempted murder of Sydney Tinkler. Suspected connection to the murder of Graball. And, most importantly of all, the very latest update on Tinkler's health. The man had, the news announcer informed his listeners, by some miracle survived the attack and was currently receiving the very best care at Banbury hospital. Although his injuries were serious and he was in a coma, his doctors saw signs for optimism and expected him to make a recovery in the coming weeks.

Dykeman had already made arrangements for a further update to be issued to the press before the six o'clock news, in the hope the BBC would include it. This would suggest that Tinkler's doctors had already spotted signs of recovery and believed it possible he would be conscious within a matter of days. If the killer hadn't been pushed into action by the initial report, surely they would be by this second bulletin. At the very least, anticipated Dykeman, they would feel obliged to check out the accuracy of the reports.

The two policemen had already inspected the arrangements made by the medical staff, with assistance from two police constables, and, having heard the announcement at one o'clock, they made their way back to the room housing Tinkler's body. There were final preparations to complete.

Rather than putting Tinkler into one of the main, public wards, which Dykeman judged would make things overly complex both for themselves and the killer, the body had been placed into a single occupancy side room. It was a large space, roughly twenty feet square, with a single window that looked out over a group of outbuildings used for storage purposes. Quiet and well away from the busier parts of the hospital, it also had the advantage of its own bathroom, which Dykeman and Shapes intended to use as their observation post. By arranging for the single bed to be moved across the room, so the headboard was up against the right-hand wall, and leaving the bathroom door ajar, you finished up with a good view of the bed and its dead occupant from inside the bathroom. All that needed to be added to complete the arrangements was a chair for use by whoever was on duty and it was job done.

Dykeman surveyed the room one last time, anxious to make sure they hadn't missed some little detail that might prove crucial. Everything looked shipshape and ready for a bedside visit by the killer. The Inspector had even started to feel a little bit excited at the prospect of what he hoped would follow.

"Can you imagine how surprised they're going to be when one of us springs at them from the bathroom? They won't know what's hit them until it's too late," said Dykeman, standing with his hands on his hips.

"That's if we've not nodded off by then," grumbled Shapes. He had his doubts about the part of the scheme that involved him spending time sat on the chair in the bathroom, bored and trying hard not to nod off. He was also increasingly of the view that it was all too complicated. Was the killer really going to fall for it?

"Cynicism, Shapes?"

"You really reckon this is going to work? Think the killer won't smell a rat?"

"It will work, Shapes. Don't you worry about that. How can it not?"

Shapes didn't answer. Instead, the two men walked across the room to take a closer look at Tinkler. He'd been laid out in the bed just as if he was still amongst the land of the living but in need of some serious medical attention. Equipment was bunched around the far end of the bed, tubes connected to the corpse in the normal way any patient would be. Dykeman was absolutely confident that, from the doorway at least, it was impossible to make out anything in the least bit suspicious. Even close up, as he and Shapes now were, it simply looked as though Tinkler was sleeping. He doubted it would have been possible to do a better job.

"Look at that," the Inspector prompted. "Tinkler's fast asleep in his coma. A man brutally attacked and now on the mend. A few more days and he'll be able to tell the world who it was tried to kill him. Perfect."

"Don't you think he looks a bit pale? Sort of deathly pale?"

"Of course he's pale, he's nearly died and lost a lot of blood. He's a man doing his best to hang on in there, resting while his body recovers. I've seen you looking worse some mornings."

Shapes mumbled something Dykeman couldn't hear, then leaned in close to Tinkler, sniffing at him.

"Smells dead to me," he declared, sulkily.

"What do you think the killer is going to do? Sneak in here, tip-toe over to the bed then have a good old sniff at Tinkler before deciding whether or not to finish him off?"

"Just saying. He smells dead."

"Point acknowledged, Shapes. Now, who's taking the first stint on surveillance?"

"Two hours?"

"As we agreed."

"I'll do it. Might as well get it out of the way."

"Good. I was hoping we'd agree on that. Means I can get myself some grub from the hospital canteen. Should set me up nicely for my first stint on duty. Now then, remember, whoever's standing guard outside the room will clear off every thirty minutes, regular as clockwork. That's when you'll need to be at your most alert. Shouldn't take our killer long to work things out and nip in the next time the coast is clear."

"I still think we should be armed," grumbled Shapes. "Could get hurt trying to disarm this killer."

"Try throwing a towel over them. Right then, I'll leave you to it. It's PC Gribbins on duty for the rest of the day. And don't fall asleep."

Having left the unhappy Shapes to twiddle his thumbs for the next two hours, Dykeman walked across the hallway to the room opposite. This was to be used as the hideout for whoever was on duty, as back-up. They'd spend some time in there themselves, swapping with two constables who'd been keen as mustard to join their little party. Dykeman had wondered if that didn't have more to do with the proximity of lots of nurses than genuine enthusiasm for the case.

The room was almost identical to the one in which they'd placed Tinkler, although it had been equipped with tea-making facilities and a small supply of reading material. If they were lucky, they wouldn't have to spend more than the one night waiting for the killer to show up. On the other hand, if their culprit was smart and had the nerve for it, they might string things out, giving themselves plenty of time to assess the situation and maximise their chances of striking undetected.

Dykeman was aware that the longer things went on, the more likely it was those on duty would get careless, maybe even nod off at precisely the wrong moment. For the first time since he'd dreamed up the scheme, the Inspector felt a little uneasy, his confidence weakening just a tad. Before his nerves had the chance to get the better of him, Dykeman turned tail and fled in the direction of the canteen, keen to both fuel up for the wait and to take his mind off the thought of anything going wrong.

DYKEMAN HAD ALREADY swapped places with Shapes for the first time at three-thirty and was back for his second stint at seven-thirty. Lord Almighty, it had been hard getting through the first shift. His dinner of liver and mashed potato, followed by apple crumble and custard, had settled happily in his stomach, then proceeded to encourage him towards sleep. After forty minutes, he'd been forced to resort to splashing water on his face and standing up; sitting down having become too risky. If Shapes got back to find him sleeping, he'd never hear the last of it.

As it turned out, Shapes tip-toed back into the side room before flinging the bathroom door wide open without warning. He seemed to Dykeman disappointed he hadn't found his boss asleep on the job.

Dykeman studiously avoided eating a hearty meal before his second stint, but did make sure he downed a large mug of coffee. He also took a book with him, *Treasure Island* by Robert Louis Stevenson. Not his normal sort of thing, but the choice had been rubbish. As with the earlier stint, the minutes crawled by as if caught in some kind of time vacuum. Ten pages of his book were read, then twenty, then thirty. Dykeman couldn't cope with any more after that, so he sat there picking at his nails and listening to the few sounds that his ears could pick up from outside the room. Already he wasn't looking forward to being there in the small hours of the morning, when he felt sure he'd not be able to stop himself from nodding off.

When eventually nine-thirty arrived, along with the grumpy figure of Shapes, Dykeman decided they needed to make an alteration to their original plan. There was no way they were going to last the first night with their existing shift-pattern. Shapes put up no resistance when Dykeman suggested they line up a couple of constables to cover the morning hours, between one-thirty and seventy-thirty. Dykeman would take up the baton from there and they'd return to their two shifts. Leaving a happier-looking Shapes with his *Racing Post*, a mug of tea and a packet of biscuits, Dykeman set off to collar some volunteers at the police station. The chance to earn a few quid extra for working overtime ought to make things easier. At least then he'd have just one more stint to do before he could clear off back home and get some decent sleep in his own bed. Bliss.

THE PLANNED UPDATE on Tinkler's much-improved condition had duly been announced on the six o'clock news that first evening, which left Dykeman feeling a little more confident about his plan than he might otherwise have been. All the same, he'd toyed with the idea of releasing a third update the following morning, maybe even going so far as to say that Tinkler had briefly regained consciousness during the night, but decided in the end that might be taking things a bit too far. The story had to remain credible.

Instead, he went straight back to the hospital in time to take over from Constable Dartington at seven-thirty, there having been no sign of anything suspicious since he'd left for home six hours earlier. Dartington looked exhausted, dark shadows under his half-closed eyes. Thank God for that, thought Dykeman, in no doubt at all he wouldn't have lasted the night if it had been his turn.

And thus the pattern from the previous evening began to repeat itself. Two-hour stretches of total boredom were shared between Dykeman and Shapes, interspersed with eating, sleeping and, in the case of Shapes, attempting to chat up one of the nurses, a large blonde woman whose response was to keep treading on his feet. Eventually, the pain got too much for Shapes and he gave up the attempt.

Dinner for the patients was served between noon and one, a highly-efficient operation that reminded Shapes of army life. So did the rubbish quality of the food. He thought it likely some of the patients would feel worse in the afternoon than they had before putting away their grub. The tea trolley followed, then a brief lull in activity. Shapes took a turn round the car park just before quarter-past one, hoping some fresh air would help him get through his next shift from one-thirty. The sun was out, warm on his skin, and the birds were singing. It was a lovely day and didn't that just make the prospect of another two hours in that bathroom all the more appealing?

Dykeman, on the other hand, was looking forward to a spot of dinner when the time came himself. It was way past his normal eating time and his stomach had been complaining often and loudly. He almost knocked Shapes over in his haste to get out of the damned room and head off in search of food.

Wandering through the main building about an hour and a half later, in search of some sort of entertainment, Dykeman realised the number of people around the place had increased markedly. Questioning the next nurse he bumped into, he established it was the start of visiting time. There would be bunches of grapes and bananas as far as the eye could see in no time at all and bored-looking people sitting on uncomfortable chairs next to their nearest and dearest, who knew they didn't really want to be there. He poked his head into a number of the wards, amused at the repeated scene of general unhappiness.

And it was as he watched a young man reading a newspaper, sitting in a chair alongside an old woman dozing in a bed next to him, that the realisation hit him. Of course. Why hadn't he thought of that. Not sure whether to be worried or delighted, he turned around and walked as fast as he could in the direction of Shapes and Sydney Tinkler. If he wasn't mistaken, the very best time for the killer to make another attempt on Tinkler's life would be when the hospital was at its busiest, which happened to be right then, during visiting time.

Nursing a throbbing knee he'd whacked against a trolley being pushed along a corridor by a distracted porter, Dykeman pulled up outside Tinkler's room, both to catch his breath and to have a listen before opening the door, just in case events were already afoot. Silence. He opened the door with care and peeked through into the brightly-lit room. Tinkler was still there, immobile in bed and apparently unmolested. Excellent, he wasn't too late. Remembering to close the door behind him, Dykeman entered the room, noticing a faint, though unpleasant smell. It seemed Tinkler was beginning to deteriorate. That was unfortunate. Another twenty-four hours, perhaps, and the smell might be so bad as to put an end to his cunning scheme. It was hard to imagine the killer sneaking into the room without noticing a stench coming from the supposedly sleeping figure of Tinkler. They would have to hope his hunch about when the killer would be most likely to strike turned out to be right.

Shapes saw Dykeman and pushed the door to the bathroom wide open.

"Wasn't expecting you yet, sir. Can't stay away?" He noticed with disappointment that his boss hadn't thought to bring him a fresh cup of tea.

"I've had an idea, Shapes."

"Oh, yes. And what might that be?"

"If you were this here killer, when would be the best time to make an attempt on Tinkler's life, here in the hospital?"

"In about another week's time, when we've all got too bored and too tired to keep ourselves awake, I reckon."

Shapes yawned and stretched his arms out in front of him, thinking perhaps it wouldn't take anything like as long as a week for that to happen. Another twenty-four hours would probably be enough.

"You have a point there, Shapes, except Tinkler will stink to high heaven by then."

"You've notice the whiff?"

"Yes. Good job I don't think he's going to be needed much longer," replied Dykeman, wondering what was happening inside Tinkler's body as it lay there on the bed. "For my money, the ideal time to strike will be when the place is really busy. That way you've got a chance of getting around unnoticed. And when is any hospital at its busiest?"

"On a Saturday night, just after the pubs have closed," grinned Shapes.

Dykeman chose to ignore his sergeant and instead answered his own question, "During visiting hours." He face wore a look of minor triumph, as if he'd solved some significant problem.

"See what you mean," said Shapes, the wrinkles that had appeared on his forehead a clear sign he was thinking, hard. "And when is visiting time, sir?"

"Right now, Shapes."

"Ah."

"Yes, ah, indeed. If I'm not mistaken, our killer is going to show up this afternoon. Can't see there's a better time to strike and why wait until tomorrow, when they think our comatose waiter might be ready to talk at any moment?"

Shapes was mildly impressed. He hadn't thought about visiting time and the cover it would provide. Stuck in that room, away from the main action in the hospital, you didn't get chance to notice a lot of what else was going on around you. Maybe he should have been paying more attention when he was on his previous breaks. Dykeman had a good point, when would be a better time?

"Be a bit of a squeeze, having two of us in here," observed Shapes, looking around him at the tiny room.

"I thought you could hide in the wardrobe."

"The wardrobe? At my age?" Shapes was aghast.

"Under the bed?"

"You having me on, sir?"

Dykeman's face said he was.

"Of course I am, Shapes. No, you stay here. I'm going to join the constable on duty in the other room. There's only about an hour and a half of visiting time left, so we won't have to wait long. As soon they make their move, you shout for help and grab them. We'll be here in the blink of an eye. Job done."

"You say so, sir."

"And be careful, Shapes. I don't doubt they'll be carrying some sort of weapon. I don't want you being careless and getting yourself injured. I've seen enough of this place the last two days. Don't want to be coming back to see how you're getting along after you've got yourself shot or stabbed."

"You're all heart, you are, sir."

Chapter Fifteen

There was, in fact, almost two hours left of visiting time and the minutes soon appeared to be passing at something like a snail's pace for the policemen, in much the same way they were for the unhappy visitors, sitting dutifully alongside their poorly relatives. The initially eager and alert policemen felt their energy levels flagging and their shoulders sagging.

Dykeman and PC Straiton sat in silence, too concerned about giving themselves away to risk even a few whispered exchanges. Straiton had a book on Byzantine history. Although a subject of no interest to Dykeman, he none-the-less soon found himself envious of Straiton's book. A copy of the *Express* newspaper the constable had long since discarded didn't take up more than twenty minutes of the Inspector's time, and that included a failed attempt at answering the crossword questions Straiton hadn't been able to complete.

Dykeman resorted to studying the stitching in his jacket sleeves, then counting the leaves on the tree outside the window. An hour limped by. Perhaps he'd got it wrong. Maybe the killer would prefer to creep into the building in the small hours of the morning, when there were few staff around the place. They didn't have any reason to think it was a trap, so all they needed to do was wait until the constable on duty left his post, then nip into the room and finish what they'd started. They could be out and gone in no time at all.

And what if they did suspect a trap? Why risk it? He'd assumed whoever it was didn't have the skills to tell for sure they'd left Tinkler dead as a dodo. But what if they did? They'd be sitting there at home, listening to the reports on the radio claiming Tinkler was on the mend, laughing their head off. If that was the case, he and Shapes could spend the whole week there and end up with nothing to show for it, except for a partially-decomposed murder victim. That wouldn't go down well with the Chief Inspector. And the press would have a field day.

Dykeman felt himself getting warm and couldn't stop fidgeting. Straiton ploughed on through his book. Muffled noises from elsewhere in the building leaked into the room, so quiet it was all but impossible to make out what they were. Boredom and doubt were in the ascendancy.

Dykeman had slipped into a rather welcome daydream involving his ownership of a Derby-winning thoroughbred. There he was, in the winner's enclosure wearing top hat and tails, accepting the trophy from the Queen, who was congratulating him on his fine horse. He was just about to lift the trophy when an almighty racket snapped him out of his reverie. At first he was confused, not able to recognise the room he was in, or why he was there, let alone work out what all that noise was, or where it was coming from. What bloody annoying timing it had been. The Queen. The Derby. The trophy. Damn it.

He shook his head and tried to focus. Things came back to him, piece-meal. The hospital. Straiton. Sydney Tinkler's killer. But what on earth was all that noise coming from somewhere outside the room. It took a moment longer for the source of the noise to register in Dykeman's mind. Of course, it was coming from the room where Shapes was watching over Tinkler's corpse. Where was Straiton? Damn it, just when the man was needed, he wasn't to be seen.

Struggling to overcome stiff limbs and the pins and needles in his left leg, Dykeman dragged himself up on to his feet. Blood rushed into his head, making him feel momentarily light-headed. More shouting and other sounds of disturbance came from Tinkler's room. Dykeman was sure it was Tinkler's room. He wobbled across to the door and pulled it open. Across the hallway, he could see the door to the other room was itself wide open. Giving his sleepy leg another shake, the returning blood causing pain to flame in the limb, Dykeman tumbled across the hallway and in through the open doorway. The sight he found there was, he decided at once, remarkable. There was no other word for it.

Still lying there, as if nothing in the world had changed, was the body of Sydney Tinkler. Eyes shut, mouth closed and his skin even more pale than before. However, it was apparent he had what could be referred to as visitors. Rather inconsiderate visitors, at that.

Sprawled sideways across the bed was Shapes. On his back, his head dangling over the far side of the bed and his legs flaying around on the near side, he had his arms wrapped round the torso and arms of a woman. She too was on her back, her skirt half-way up her thighs, and as she screamed blue murder, she struggled like the devil to break free from the grip of his sergeant, who was bellowing for help himself.

Sheila Louch's eyes were wide and wild, filled with hatred. And as for the industrial language that came from her mouth, well, a coal miner would be hard-pushed to match it. Her legs flew out and up, then back and out and up again, in a frenzied manner. Poor old Shapes was having quite a time keeping hold of her. Dykeman looked around. Nothing suitable to help restrain the woman. He'd just have to make a go at getting his cuffs on her. If Shapes could just keep her locked in his arms a little longer.

"I'm here, Shapes," yelled Dykeman over the screams, as he reached for his cuffs. "Keep a grip on her so I can get the cuffs on."

Sheila Louch saw him now, swinging her head to the side and looking down the length of her body. It only seemed to make her struggle all the more. Shapes said something, but Dykeman couldn't make it out. That turned out to be a little unfortunate.

"Keep her there, Shapes."

It was as he moved in close to the two combatants that he saw it for the first time. Gripped in Sheila Louch's right hand, so tight her knuckles were ivory-white, was a large kitchen knife. Dykeman hesitated, wondering how best to disarm her before he had a go at getting the cuffs on. As it happened, thinking time was up almost as soon as it started. Making one more, all-in effort to throw off Shapes's bear hug, Sheila Louch broke free, hurtling up and forward, so that she finished up in a heap on the floor beside the bed. A deep-throated howl of pain came from Shapes, who rolled on to his side and clapped a hand on his right thigh. Blood began to trickle between his fingers and, noticed Dykeman, his face had gone pale.

Sheila Louch was quicker of thought and deed than the confused Dykeman. The woman was back on her feet, hunched over in a threatening stance, the knife still in her right hand, her wild eyes boring into Dykeman. For some reason, he couldn't help thinking how much better she looked with her hair all unkempt. It was a look that suited only a select few women, of which she was clearly one.

Inching at first towards the startled and worried Inspector, then a tad to his right, Louch closed the gap little by little. Dykeman feared the worst. The woman looked demented. Talking to her wasn't likely to do much good, but he'd have to try, all the same. The taste of the chicken soup he'd had for lunch washed back into his mouth. It took some effort to stop himself from being sick.

"Now, come on Mrs Louch." The words struggled out, apparently reluctant to put in an appearance. Dykeman coughed, to help clear his throat. "There's no way out for you here. You'll only make matters worse. Why don't you give me that knife and sit down on this chair here."

Sheila Louch not only failed to reply, she didn't take her hate-filled eyes off him, continuing to inch to his right. In response, he took half a step to his left and angled his body a little towards her, so as not to allow himself to be out-flanked by that knife. She must have sensed his fears because, without warning, she thrust the knife out towards him, leaning in behind the lunge, a banshee scream exploding from her mouth.

Dykeman jumped backwards, yelling in terror. The heel of his right shoe caught on the floor and he felt himself buckle and fall. Unable to break the fall with his hands, he found himself sprawled across the ground, exposed and fully expecting Sheila Louch to put her blood-stained weapon to use once more. God, how he wished he'd not let himself get into such poor shape. Too many pies and pints and too little exercise. If he got out of this mess in one piece, he promised himself things would change.

As he rolled on to his back and pushed himself up on to his bum, Dykeman saw Shapes gamely trying to come to his aid, but the poor old sod was struggling to take any weight on his right leg, where his trousers were now stained dark with blood.

"Off him, you murdering old witch," bellowed Shapes, his face scrunched up into something out of a horror film, a mixture of pain and rage.

Sheila Louch glanced at Shapes, then back at Dykeman and, still without uttering another word, turned and fled for the door.

It could have, contemplated Dykeman some time later, turned out all very differently. Things had taken a bad enough course as it was and seemed about to get considerably worse as Sheila Louch made her bid for freedom. How fortunate, in that case, that Straiton should choose that very moment to put in an appearance. It was pure theatre, thought Dykeman, or should that be farce? As Louch bolted for the open doorway, Straiton came hurtling into the room, alerted by the furore he'd been able to hear from the gents toilets, where he'd been doing what needed doing.

Unaware of each other until it was too late, Louch and Straiton ran slap bang into each other, the superior foot speed and extra weight of the latter knocking the former backwards and off her feet. As the knife arced up through the air in the general direction of Tinkler, the two temporarily entwined figures crashed to the floor, an indeterminate tangle of arms and legs. Shapes watched as the knife landed, point first, with a soft thud, in the bed, a mere two or three inches from Tinkler's head. The sergeant raised an eyebrow.

Dykeman was back on his feet and began to help untangle the confused and dazed Straiton from the prone figure of Sheila Louch, on whom he had landed with some force.

"Well done, Straiton. Perfect timing," said the thankful Dykeman, holding the constable's arm as he regained his senses and his balance.

"What happened?" asked Straiton, looking down at Sheila Louch. "Who's she?" He stretched his back and winced with the pain. "Christ, that hurts."

"That, Straiton, is Sheila Louch. She's our killer and you, I'm very happy to say, have just stopped her from getting away. Sterling work, Straiton."

"Blimey. A woman did it." He felt the ribs on the right side of his body. They were sore. "Do you think it was her that did Henry Graball in, too?"

"I suspect it was, Straiton. Probably revenge for what he did to her husband, though we haven't found out yet why she then killed Tinkler." Dykeman bent down to take a closer look at Louch. "Looks like you knocked her out, Straiton. Good job you missed that knife of hers. Nasty-looking thing."

Straiton's face went pale and he stopped rubbing his ribs. "Knife, sir? What knife's that?"

"This one 'ere," replied Shapes, pointing towards the handle that jutted up alongside Tinkler's head. "Big one it is, too." Shapes grinned, despite the pain coming from his leg.

Straiton stared, open-mouthed.

"You didn't see it then, Straiton?" asked Shapes, wanting to laugh but worried it would make the pain too much to bear.

Straiton shook his head, still unable to speak.

Sheila Louch stirred and mumbled something incomprehensible.

"Come on, let's get her up and into that chair," ordered Dykeman. "Got your cuffs, Straiton?"

"Sir." Straiton placed a hand on the cuffs that were clipped to his belt.

"Well, best get them on her. Don't want her making another bid for freedom."

As they hauled the groggy woman up from the floor and Straiton slapped his handcuffs on her as quickly as he could, a young nurse, her eyes wide with concern, poked her head around the door. Words tried to form on her lips, but didn't quite manage it.

"Ah, nurse. Excellent timing," Dykeman said, breathing heavily with the effort of holding on to Louch as Straiton cuffed her. "Shapes there has a bit of a cut on his leg. You best have a look at the old fella before he passes out."

Shapes wanted to respond, but he was beginning to feel light-headed. He placed a hand on the side of the bed to take some of the weight off his injured leg. The nurse was with him in a flash, easing him down into a sitting position on the ground. He knew he ought to be happy as Larry to be getting such attention from a sexy young nurse, but the room was starting to go all blurry. Odd that. He hadn't had a drink all day. With that he passed out, falling into a deep slumber.

Chapter Sixteen

"Well, about bloody time, Shapes. I've been here most of the afternoon, waiting for you to wake up. Don't tell me, you've been dreaming about nurses?"

Dykeman was sitting in an uncomfortable metal-framed chair alongside the bed the nurse and a porter had carefully placed Shapes in after his return from the operating theatre. Shapes looked tired, his face pale and the lines in the skin around his neck and across his forehead more pronounced than usual. The poor old sod had lost a lot of blood. It had been a good job they were already on hospital premises, otherwise who knows what might have happened. As it was, he looked at least ten years over the fifty-three he owned up to.

Shapes struggled to open his dark-rimmed eyes, the glare of the ceiling lights too much at first. His head throbbed and he felt a peculiar dull ache in his right thigh. What had happened? And, for that matter, where was he? God, how he could do with a drink. His mouth was so dry his tongue kept sticking to the roof.

Someone was talking. The voice seemed familiar, but who was it? The words were hard to make out. Oh, why bother?

He started to drift back to sleep. It felt good; calming, warm and safe. Ah, that was it, just let himself slip back into a deep slumber. And hadn't he been dreaming? What about? He couldn't remember, but was confident it would all come back to him. Wonderful.

God, what was that? The world felt like it was moving about violently. An earthquake? Did they have earthquakes wherever he was? Bloody Nora, it was getting worse. He opened his eyes with a start, then closed them just as fast as bright burning light flooded in. He tried to shout, but the dryness in his mouth wouldn't let him. And there was that voice again. Who the hell was it? He'd give them a right piece of his mind, when he got round to it. Damn it, there was no going back to sleep now. The light glowed through his eyelids and other sounds started coming to his ears. Murmurs at first, they steadily shaped themselves into other voices. Damn it, his head hurt.

He squinted through half-closed eyelids, his eyes struggling to adjust to the brightness. He was laying down, yes he was definitely laying down and there was something big and dark to his right. He managed to lean his head over to the right an inch or so and ease his eyelids open a little more. As the blurriness began to clear, he started to get some focus. It was a person. Someone big. They were smiling and, yes, it was their voice he could hear.

"Shapes. Shapes. You in there? It's Dykeman, you old git. Come on, time to re-join the rest of us happy campers."

Dykeman? Shapes thought on the name for a moment. Dykeman. Yes, he knew that name. The thick fog that slowed his brain thinned a little and he caught a glimpse of things.

Dykeman. Yes, it was Inspector Dykeman. He worked with Dykeman, didn't he? Policemen. The hospital. There'd been a fight in the hospital and he'd been stabbed. An image of a demented woman launching herself at him, wielding a horrible great knife filled his mind. God, the woman had been terrifying and so strong. Where had she got all that strength from? He'd tried to fend her off and they'd grappled and scrapped, but she managed to stab him in the leg as they fell on to the bed. The bed? Why a bed? That was it, Sydney Tinkler.

He opened his eyes as fully as he could, still squinting in the glare of the ceiling lights. Sitting there next to him was Dykeman, his ugly big face filled with a stupid grin. What did he have to be so happy about? Where had Dykeman been when he needed him?

"That's more like it. How you feeling? Doctor said you'll be right as rain soon enough. Flesh wound, he said," lied Dykeman, happy as could be to see his sergeant's eyes open.

Shapes tried to speak, to swear some abuse at Dykeman, but his mouth was still too dry.

"Mouth dry is it? Here we go, a glass of nice, cold water for you."

Dykeman lifted the tall glass of water from the small bedside cabinet and brought it to the lips of the parched sergeant. Shapes was willing, in fact he was keen, but his mouth wouldn't open properly and most of the cold liquid he tried to swallow ran down the sides of his face and over his neck. He coughed and spluttered.

"Gone down the wrong hole, has it?" joked Dykeman.

As if from nowhere, a rotund, middle-aged nurse appeared, immediately fussing around her patient. Dykeman noticed she smelled of lavender and her hands were so big they looked better suited to a builder. He kept his observations to himself.

"Now then, Mr Shapes, you be careful or you'll go and tear those stitches in your leg."

She eased Shapes upright with such little apparent effort that Dykeman wasn't sure he could believe his eyes. After re-arranging the pillows so they better supported Shapes's wobbly head, the nurse swiped the glass of water from Dykeman's hands, leaving behind a disapproving scowl, and brought it with practised care to her patient's lips. Shapes swallowed a little of the cool liquid, delighted to feel it washing across his dry tongue and on down his throat. He had downed half the contents of the glass before he weakly nodded at the nurse to say he'd had his fill.

"That's better," the nurse declared, before turning to face Dykeman. "Now don't you go wearing out Mr Shapes. By rights, he should be left all alone to sleep right now, so soon after his operation."

"Understood, nurse." Dykeman quivered inside under the intense stare of the nurse and considered himself properly told off, though what for he wasn't exactly sure. Still, best not to question these things, if his experience of bossy women was anything to go by.

"Ten minutes, then you're off," declared Nurse Curse, as her name badge informed Dykeman. "You can always come back tomorrow. I'm sure Mr Shapes will be much better by then, won't you, Mr Shapes?"

He might have been feeling poorly and slow in the head, but Shapes too recognised the voice of authority when he heard it and his head moved slowly backward and forward, twice to indicate his acknowledgement.

"Blimey, you've got a right one there, Shapes," chuckled Dykeman as he watched the large bottom of Nurse Curse wobble off in the direction of another patient. "Never know, she might pay you a private visit in the night, when everyone else is asleep."

Shapes closed his eyes. If he could have managed the effort, he would have pleaded to be taken home at once. His boss was enjoying things far too much. He ran his tongue over his lips before trying to speak.

"Mrs Louch." The words were strained, as difficult to speak as they were for Dykeman to hear. Shapes tried again. "Mrs Louch. What happened?"

"The wicked witch of Banbury, as the men down the station are calling her?" Dykeman leaned in closer to his sergeant and lowered his voice. Best not to let any of the other people on the ward hear anything they didn't need to hear. "Got her under lock and key down the station right now. Straiton did a grand job taking her out like that. I was getting worried she might get clean away, what with her being armed with that nasty looking knife she shoved in your leg."

Shapes glanced down the bed, wondering what kind of a mess lay under the sheets, then decided he could wait until later to find out the answer. Stitches, the nurse had said. It must be serious. Maybe life-threatening.

Dykeman plucked a plump red grape from the bunch he'd brought along, eyed it carefully, then popped it in his mouth and crushed it between his teeth before swallowing. Decent flavour, he decided.

"The doctor wouldn't let us speak to her until he'd finished his examination, in case she was suffering from concussion. Apparently even a killer has to have the best medical treatment available and the law can wait its turn. Anyway, he declared her fit enough to face a few questions, so I got on with it; not that it took much effort. She owned up to the lot. Killed Graball after what he did to her old man. Said she couldn't stand the thought of him getting away with ruining their lives like that. He laughed at them, rubbed their noses in it, just like he did with all the others. She knew her husband didn't have what it took to kill a man, so she did it herself. That was the real reason they agreed to go to Graball's party. She hoped she'd get a chance to murder him and, what with there being so many other people there, she reckoned she might get away with it. Tough old bird. Didn't regret a bit of it. Said she loved the look on Graball's face when he realised his time was up."

Dykeman picked off a second grape, studied it closely, as he did with the first, then despatched it in the same way.

"Tinkler?" came the barely audible prompt from Shapes.

"Tinkler? Ah, that's another matter altogether. It was her alright. She owned up to that too. But he wasn't part of her plans. Sod's Law kicked in. How many times have we seen that before?"

Dykeman paused as he watched an old, wrinkly skinned man with an oxygen mask on his face being pushed towards the exit doors in a wheelchair, which squeaked and clumped as it trundled along. The poor old fella looked like he was on his last legs. Probably wouldn't get to see the outside world again. It sent a shiver up the Inspector's spine. God forbid the day came when he finished up like that. Hospitals. Glum places. He brought his attention back to Shapes.

"Where was I? I was telling you about Tinkler. Well, it turns out he saw Sheila Louch leaving the office where Henry Graball was murdered. Told her he was suspicious what she'd been up to, because she looked all bothered, and would have taken a look in the room if not for the fact he was carrying a large pile of dirty plates to the kitchens. He decided he'd take a look on his way back, but when the alarm went up, he didn't get a chance."

Dykeman paused as a nurse arrived to check on the middle-aged patient sleeping in the bed behind him. Seemingly content all was well, she moved on elsewhere.

"Anyway, it was only when he heard about Graball having been murdered that he must have put two and two together and realised it was Sheila Louch who did it. That was why she looked so nervous coming out of the office. Next thing she knows, Tinkler turns up at their house when hubby is out and makes his demands for keeping his silence. Said she tried to bluff it, but he wasn't having any of that. Goes without saying, he wanted money, lots of it, but he also demanded sexual favours. That was a step too far for the woman. Hardly surprising she didn't much fancy crawling into bed with that man, especially given the state of that house of his. So she decided in for a penny, in for a pound. After a bit of off-the-cuff thinking, she agreed to meet him at his place, where she promptly smashed him over the head with a hammer. Said she was properly surprised when she heard on the radio Tinkler wasn't dead. Apparently she didn't hold anything back when she hit him."

Dykeman plucked another grape, chewed on it, then swallowed, savouring its sweet taste.

"Nice and sweet these grapes. Well, we've got the woman under lock and key down the station now. Shouldn't have too much trouble getting a conviction for both murders, not after she volunteered such a fulsome confession." Dykeman gave a little chuckle. "Should have seen the look on her face when I told her Tinkler was already dead before she tried to stab him here. She went pale as a ghost. Ah, I reckon they'll put this one in the training books for new recruits. We'll be role models for years to come, Shapes."

"That's good," whispered Shapes.

"Think I'm looking forward to my next press briefing. Make a nice change, will that."

The effort required to concentrate on what Dykeman was saying, let alone making his own minor contributions, left Shapes feeling drained. He closed his eyes and felt his whole body sag, which was something of a surprise given his already horizontal position in bed. At least they'd got their killer, that was good. But now he wouldn't mind a little sleep. Just a nap.

Nurse Curse must have possessed the eyesight of a hawk, decided Dykeman, because, despite being occupied with another patient on the opposite side of the ward, she apparently noticed Shapes slipping back to dreamland and swept across the room to take another close look at her patient.

"Right, you," she barked at Dykeman, who instantly shifted uncomfortably in his chair. "Visiting time is over. Mr Shapes needs his rest and he won't get that while he's being pestered by you. So, off you go. I'm sure he'll be happy enough to see you again tomorrow."

The words were accompanied by an icy stare and Dykeman was on his feet in a flash, less than keen to find out what would happen to him if he malingered, even for mere seconds.

As he strolled out of the building and into a warm afternoon, filled with bright sunlight, filtering through the leaves of the tall chestnut trees that lined that side of the building, Dykeman felt a deep sense of satisfaction rise within him. They'd not done bad at all, especially when you think how many potential suspects there were in the Conservative Club when Graball was murdered. He wasn't sure he could recall ever having been involved before in a case like it. And then there'd been the murder of Tinkler. That one could have tripped them up. Quite a stroke of genius as it turned out, if he said so himself, to come up with the idea of using Tinkler to flush out the killer. And when she did show herself, she could hardly have been more helpful, even if she didn't realise at first what the truth of things was. Yes, it had all turned out very nicely. Well, apart from the little flesh wound Shapes had suffered. But once he'd had a decent kip, he'd love being in there with all those nurses; though perhaps not so much Nurse Curse.

Chapter Seventeen

Dykeman and Shapes stood together outside the Oxford Assizes a month later, taking the trouble to detach themselves from the gaggle of people who'd made their way on to the street. A fine drizzle that had been falling for most of the day had almost at once begun to add a gentle sheen to their hats and coats. The chat amongst the public seemed to Dykeman to be a little disappointed. This didn't altogether surprise him. The prosecution against Sheila Louch had been a simple matter, what with her pleading guilty, and the judge had wasted no time in dishing out the death sentence, much to the delight of most of those in the court room. However, it seemed many of them had been hoping the case would spend longer in court, no doubt so they could hear more of the gory details, thought Dykeman.

Louch left the court in silence, her head down. Dykeman had noticed how pale and tired she looked, nothing like the wild-eyed maniac who'd attacked him, Shapes and Straiton. It was, he contemplated, as if she'd long since seen the writing on the wall and had been simply awaiting the inevitable.

"Glad to see she'll swing for it," said Shapes as he pulled the raised collar of his coat closer to his face.

"Would have gone for stoning, myself," replied Dykeman.

"Eh?"

Shapes looked into his superior's eyes with considerable surprise. Dykeman was hardly known for being a supporter of capital punishment. Was he on the mend?

Dykeman shook his head. "You should go and chat with that disgruntled lot over there," he went on, nodding towards a group of people who had brought their campaign for an end to the death penalty to the street outside the court. "Sounds like they don't have quite the same view of things as you do."

Shapes snarled at the protestors. "Should be locked up, that lot. You murder someone then you deserve to swing. They should try talking to the relatives of murder victims. That would soon change their minds."

Dykeman glanced at his watch. He wasn't keen on repeating a conversation he'd had with Shapes many a time before and, anyway, his sergeant had an appointment. It was already gone three, which didn't leave Shapes all that much time to get back to Banbury.

"You'd better get going if you want to catch the twenty-five past three train. Show up late for your check-up and you'll have Nurse Curse after you. I bet you've been missing her, haven't you." Dykeman grinned.

"Sod off. She's mad as a spoon, that woman. Did I tell you what she did when I spilled some of my soup on the bed?"

"You did, Shapes. Twice, as it happens."

"Made me wear a bib. Felt like a bloody baby, I did." He spoke like a man forced to bear a cross of humiliation for the rest of his life.

"So you said. Anyway, you can't fool me. You loved all that attention. And from all them nurses too."

"Well, the other nurses weren't so bad, I'll grant you. But her. I couldn't sleep proper at night wondering when she might sneak up on me next."

Dykeman chuckled. On one of his visits to the hospital to see Shapes, his sergeant had begged him to help him escape. Said he'd tried excusing himself, but Nurse Curse wasn't having it. She'd bundled him back into bed and warned him she'd give him a sound spanking if he tried it again. Ah, the thought of Shapes being bent over the woman's knee. What a hoot.

The crowd had begun to thin out, people put off lingering any longer by the drizzle. The reporters had practically sprinted from the building the second the sentence was announced. They had deadlines to meet and impatient news editors to keep happy.

"I'm going to make my way back to Banbury later, Shapes. You might as well head home after your check-up. Nothing left to do back at the station today."

Shapes eyed Dykeman with suspicion. What was he up to?

"Got a date, have you?"

Dykeman coughed. If it was intended to be in anyway distracting, then it failed miserably.

"You have, haven't you?" pressed Shapes, wagging a finger. "You sly old thing."

"I'm having afternoon tea with Dr Delph at the Churchill Hotel."

"Blimey, gone all posh have you? She's paying, I suppose? You couldn't afford to eat a packet of crisps there."

"We're going to split the bill." Dykeman looked sheepish and had started to wish he'd left already.

"Got a room upstairs too, have you? Bet you've not told her that part yet."

Shapes nudged Dykeman's arm and laughed like the dirty old man the Inspector often took him to be.

Just as Dykeman went to tell his sergeant where to go, a man and woman stepped out of the court entrance arm-in-arm. With barely a glance to see who might still be there, they turned and hurried off up the road, away from the two policemen. Dykeman nodded in their direction.

"Phillip Underwood and Daphne Graball, scuttling away before someone sees them."

Shapes turned round just in time to catch a glimpse of the two fleeing figures before they disappeared down a side street. He grinned.

"Right old scandal, him leaving his wife and taking up with the widow," said Shapes, with more than a hint of amusement in his voice. "And so soon. You'd have thought they'd leave it longer than a month."

"So runs the course of true love, Shapes. You should know."
"What?"

"Suppose it'll be wedding bells next. Once Underwood has got himself a divorce. Anyway, Shapes, if you don't get a move on, you'll miss that train. Go on, clear off. I'll see you at the station in the morning. You can tell me all about your night of passion with Nurse Curse."

"I'd rather snog a baboon's backside than spend a night with that woman."

Dykeman laughed so much it hurt his sides.

AFTERNOON TEA WITH Sheila Delph had been an absolute pleasure. She was one woman who never seemed to mind his little peculiarities. And he always found, or nearly always, that he could talk to her without tripping over his own tongue. Even when he talked what he felt sure was utter rubbish, or fell into the trap of starting a discussion about something he knew full well she wasn't interested in, she never seemed bothered. Mind you, he had noticed, eventually, how skilled she was at steering any such conversation on to an alternative subject with a remarkable degree of tact.

It was true that the Churchill was more upmarket than the usual sort of establishment he frequented, but Sheila Delph had been keen on it, so he agreed after only a little persuasion. All the same, he hadn't felt properly comfortable there among all those toffs and deep-pocketed tourists who poured in from all corners of the world to marvel at the wonder of the City of Dreaming Spires. Mind you, the cakes. Blimey, they were the work of a genius. Tasted like nothing he'd ever had before. By the time he started munching his way through his fourth, he was casting furtive glances to all corners to see if anyone was looking on disapproving. Sheila had laughed. Not in an unfriendly way. More a sort of delight at seeing him enjoying himself.

Been a shame in the end that it hadn't gone on longer, but Sheila needed to be in London for an evening engagement. Some horrific-sounding lecture on recent research into the effect of fatty foods on the arteries. He didn't even care to think about that. Might risk putting him off his full English breakfast down the station canteen.

As he watched her train pull out of the station, Dykeman felt a little wistful. Delph waved to him from the window, then ducked back inside to avoid risk of decapitation. He'd never really felt quite the same about any other woman and he wasn't entirely sure, as yet, just what his feelings were towards Sheila Delph, but something tugged and nagged at him as he found himself standing there, feeling alone, on a platform populated by dozens of other people. But there wasn't time to dwell. His own train was due in shortly and he needed to cross the bridge to the opposite platform. Still, he couldn't help wondering, as he made his way along the platform, just how Sheila felt about him.

IT WAS LATER THAN HE'D intended when Dykeman sat down for his tea. He'd decided to forgo the formalities of eating at the dinner table. He could slob it whenever he liked, really. After all, it wasn't as if there was anyone else there to complain about his lack of manners.

He eased his aching body into his favourite armchair, careful to keep a firm grip on the plate he'd piled high with his tea of steak and kidney pie, chips and peas, picked up from the nearby chippie on his way home from the train station. They didn't do the best chips in town, but they weren't bad. He reached down beside the chair with an outstretched hand and picked up the ketchup bottle, before emptying big dollops of the red stuff over his food.

He pushed a couple of warm, ketchup-soaked chips into his mouth and started to chew. Ah, what could beat pie and chips for dinner at the end of a long, knackering day? Damned if he knew an answer to that one. Probably nothing could. His knife cut into the pie and the rich aroma of steak and kidney wafted up his nostrils. Heaven.

For the briefest of moments, the image of Sheila Louch launching herself at him with that knife flitted into his mind. Yes, he'd not exactly put up much of a fight, had he? Things could have turned out very differently if not for Straiton showing up when he did. Stroke of luck, was that. He looked down at the pie, hesitated, then decided he would start work on getting himself into some sort of half-decent shape the following morning. Well, there was no point in letting good food go to waste, was there?

As the last of his dinner settled heavily in his stomach, Dykeman slid the empty plate on to the floor and picked up his copy of *The Vegetable Grower's Handbook* by Arthur Simons. It was his favourite book about growing vegetables and much more pleasurable to read than any novel. He was revisiting the advice on growing cabbages, a row of which had been giving him trouble in his own garden. If they didn't get a move on soon, there'd be nothing to them come harvest time.

Apart from the classical music that was barely more than a murmur from the radio, there was not a sound to be heard and the modest fire he'd lit had already filled the room with a pleasing warm glow. Dykeman opened the book, then rested it against his rotund stomach.

He'd hoped to speak to Wendy Slip again. He still wondered at her real feelings towards Henry Graball. Everyone else reckoned she was only after his money. Not an unreasonable suspicion, he had to admit. But he'd never been entirely convinced about that. He couldn't let go of the notion that she really had been in love with the man, despite everything everyone else said about him. And, there seemed to be no doubt about it, Henry Graball had not always treated his fellow man in a way that you could describe as friendly or considerate. Selfish, heartless and vindictive were words that had cropped up often in reference to him throughout their investigations.

But it looked like he'd missed his chance to try again to work out if Slip really had been in love with the man. It had come to their attention, from the ever observant personage of Anne Nettle, that Wendy Slip had taken up with Owen Plenty, who had decided to shut up shop in Banbury and start over again in the West Country. Slip and Plenty, apparently, had already spent time down in Devon and Cornwall, scouting out potential new premises. He might have got to have a word with her, if she'd been needed at court, but once it became clear she wouldn't, she'd opted to stay away and avoid a potential scene with Daphne Graball.

Oh well, there was nothing to be done about that. Funny thing was, he could see Plenty and Slip making a decent couple. Certainly more of a future in it for Slip than with the much older and totally self-centred Graball.

Word had also started filtering through that Graball Enterprises, or whatever it was called, was going to be broken up and sold off. Neither of the Graball children was interested in taking it on and there seemed little alternative. Certainly, Daphne Graball had no interest in running her dead husband's business empire. Just imagine, mused Dykeman, all that effort by Graball. Years and years of toil, back-stabbing and ruthlessly doing away with the opposition and, in next to no time, nothing would be left to show for it. It made you think.

Graball's funeral had been one of the events of the year in Banbury. The whole of Oxfordshire, in fact. The same faces they'd seen at the Conservative Club for his anniversary party had shown up at the cemetery; no doubt more concerned about reasserting their position in the town's social hierarchy than in showing their respects for a man who had treated most of them badly.

He and Shapes had watched from a distance, sheltering under their umbrellas from the heavy rain that fell from the dark, grumpy-looking skies. Graball's will had set out the requirements for his funeral in remarkable detail, including the construction of an enormous stone building that was to act as a permanent reminder to the town of the great man that had once graced them with his presence. It was the kind of self-obsessed act they'd come to expect of the man. Construction of the mausoleum had started only the previous day.

He hadn't been able to make his mind up about Matthew Louch. The funny thing was, he hadn't seemed altogether surprised when they told him what his wife had been up to, or at least not as far as the killing of Henry Graball was concerned. He had continued to claim he knew nothing about her plans and they'd not been able to put together a case against him, but Dykeman still wondered if the wife had really been able to keep things entirely secret from her husband. Still, whether he did or not, his public announcement that he would remain faithful to his wife and visit her in prison until her hanging had been quite moving. Or, it had been to most people. Shapes declared him to be a lunatic who should dump his murderous wife as soon as he could, then get on his bike and find himself a new, younger model. Ever the romantic, was Shapes.

Dykeman's eyes had closed. The warmth from the fire, the food in his belly and his favourite armchair. The perfect combination. He began to think again about Sheila Delph. That smile of hers. Quite a decent backside, too. Maybe Shapes had been right after all with his sarcastic comments about going on a date.

He didn't notice the book tip forward then slip from his lap and drop to the floor with a gentle bump. He was asleep by then, already dreaming of enormous cabbages, sweet tasting strawberries and runner beans in such abundance he would still be eating them come Christmas.

BEN WESTERHAM

The End

THE CLUB OF DEATH

The Hobby Horse Murder

If you've enjoyed reading *The Club of Death* then why not take a look at the third story in the series *The Hobby Horse Murder*. https://benwesterham.com/books/book-details-the-hobby-horse-murder/

Free Book

IF YOU ENJOYED MEETING Dykeman and Shapes then why not find out how it all began as they investigate their very first murder case together. Download your free copy of *Murder at Stockton Farm*, sit back, relax and enjoy yourself as bruised egos and repeated misunderstandings ensure that solving the case isn't the only challenge the two policemen will need to overcome before the day is done.

https://benwesterham.com/bookoffer/

THE CLUB OF DEATH

If you enjoyed this book then please consider leaving a review
at the store you bought it from.
Many thanks,
Ben Westerham

From The David Good private investigator series

From 'Good Investigations'

"MR GOOD," SHE PURRED like a hungry cat meeting a blind mouse, "and I do hope you will be." She slid beautifully, effortlessly in to the knackered old punter's chair, and I swear the thing wrapped itself lovingly around her sexy, lithe frame. Then she tempted me with those dark bewitching eyes, calling me closer, closer, closer

From 'Good Girl Gone Bad'

IF YOU ASK ME, GOOD girls can be the baddest there are, if the fancy takes them. Maybe it's because they save it all up for one big splurge, then go mad bad. I don't know, but what I do know is that anyone who tries telling you some little darling of theirs' wouldn't say boo to a goose is either stupid, misinformed or both. Any goody two shoes type should carry a health warning, 'Danger, Good Girl. May go bad at any moment'.

From the Alexander Templeman espionage series

From 'The House of Spies'

MY FINGERS WERE TINGLING from the force of the blow and my head pounding as my heart beat madly. I was exhilarated. There is no other way to put it, such was my sense of excitement at what I had just done. But there was also an edge of fear now over what I had started and the knowledge that there was no going back, no means of trying to explain away my assault as some sort of unfortunate accident. I was committed to a course of action, with no guarantee of success and no real idea of the consequences of failure, other than they would not be good.

BEN WESTERHAM

You can find out more about Ben Westerham here
www.benwesterham.com[1].

1. http://www.benwesterham.com/